DATE DUE

DE 17 '02			

DEMCO 38-296

THE
WOMAN WHO
WAS CHANGED

and Other Stories

PEARL S. BUCK

THE
WOMAN WHO
WAS CHANGED

and Other Stories

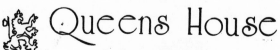

Larchmont, New York

To the Reader
To aid catalogers and collectors, this title is
printed in an edition limited to 150 copies.

QUEENS HOUSE
Larchmont, New York 10538

BOOKS ARE WEAPONS IN THE WAR OF IDEAS

Manufactured in
the United States
of America

BY PEARL S. BUCK

Fiction

EAST WIND: WEST WIND, 1930
THE GOOD EARTH, 1931
SONS, 1932
THE FIRST WIFE AND OTHER
    STORIES, 1933
THE MOTHER, 1934
A HOUSE DIVIDED, 1935
HOUSE OF EARTH [*trilogy of*
    The Good Earth, *revised,*
    Sons *and* A House Divided],
    1935
THIS PROUD HEART, 1938
THE PATRIOT, 1939
OTHER GODS, 1941
TODAY AND FOREVER, 1941
DRAGON SEED, 1942
THE PROMISE, 1943
PORTRAIT OF A MARRIAGE, 1945
THE TOWNSMAN [as John
    Sedges], 1945
PAVILION OF WOMEN, 1946
THE ANGRY WIFE [as John
    Sedges], 1947
FAR AND NEAR: STORIES OF
    JAPAN, CHINA, AND AMERICA,
    1947
PEONY, 1948
KINFOLK, 1949
THE LONG LOVE
    [as John Sedges], 1949

GOD'S MEN, 1951
BRIGHT PROCESSION [as John
    Sedges], 1952
THE HIDDEN FLOWER, 1952
VOICES IN THE HOUSE
    [as John Sedges], 1953
COME, MY BELOVED, 1953
IMPERIAL WOMAN, 1956
LETTER FROM PEKING, 1957
COMMAND THE MORNING, 1959
FOURTEEN STORIES, 1961
A BRIDGE FOR PASSING, 1962
THE LIVING REED, 1963
DEATH IN THE CASTLE, 1965
THE TIME IS NOON, 1967
THE NEW YEAR, 1968
THE GOOD DEED, 1969
THE THREE DAUGHTERS OF
    MADAME LIANG, 1969
MANDALA, 1970
THE GODDESS ABIDES, 1972
ALL UNDER HEAVEN, 1973
THE RAINBOW, 1974
EAST AND WEST, 1975
SECRETS OF THE HEART, 1976
THE LOVERS AND OTHER
    STORIES, 1977
THE WOMAN WHO WAS
    CHANGED AND OTHER
    STORIES, 1979

Translation

ALL MEN ARE BROTHERS [SHUI HU CHUAN], 1933

General

IS THERE A CASE FOR FOREIGN
    MISSIONS? [*pamphlet*], 1932
THE EXILE, 1936
FIGHTING ANGEL, 1936

MY SEVERAL WORLDS, 1954
FRIEND TO FRIEND, with Carlos
    P. Romulo, 1958
THE JOY OF CHILDREN, 1964

THE CHINESE NOVEL, 1939
OF MEN AND WOMEN, 1941
AMERICAN UNITY AND ASIA, 1942
WHAT AMERICA MEANS TO ME, 1943
THE SPIRIT AND THE FLESH [combining The Exile and Fighting Angel], 1944
TALK ABOUT RUSSIA, with Masha Scott, 1945
TELL THE PEOPLE, 1945
HOW IT HAPPENS: TALK ABOUT THE GERMAN PEOPLE, 1914–1933, with Erna von Pustau, 1947
AMERICAN ARGUMENT, with Eslanda Goode Robeson, 1949
THE CHILD WHO NEVER GREW, 1950

CHILDREN FOR ADOPTION, 1965
THE GIFTS THEY BRING, with Gweneth T. Zarfoss, 1965
FOR SPACIOUS SKIES: JOURNEY IN DIALOGUE, with Theodore F. Harris, 1966
TO MY DAUGHTERS, WITH LOVE, 1967
CHINA AS I SEE IT, 1970
THE KENNEDY WOMEN, 1970
THE STORY BIBLE, 1971
CHINA: PAST AND PRESENT, 1972
A COMMUNITY SUCCESS STORY, with Elisabeth Waechter, 1972
ONCE UPON A CHRISTMAS, 1972
PEARL BUCK'S ORIENTAL COOKBOOK, 1972
WORDS OF LOVE, 1974

Juvenile

THE YOUNG REVOLUTIONIST, 1932
STORIES FOR LITTLE CHILDREN, 1940
THE CHINESE CHILDREN NEXT DOOR, 1942
THE WATER-BUFFALO CHILDREN, 1943
THE DRAGON FISH, 1944
YU LAN: FLYING BOY OF CHINA, 1945
THE BIG WAVE, 1948
THE BIG FIGHT, 1965
THE LITTLE FOX IN THE MIDDLE, 1966
MATTHEW, MARK, LUKE AND JOHN, 1967

ONE BRIGHT DAY, 1950
THE MAN WHO CHANGED CHINA: THE STORY OF SUN YAT-SEN, 1953
JOHNNY JACK AND HIS BEGINNINGS, 1954
THE BEECH TREE, 1955
CHRISTMAS MINIATURE, 1957
MY SEVERAL WORLDS [Abridged for Younger Readers], 1957
THE CHRISTMAS GHOST, 1960
WELCOME CHILD, 1964
THE CHINESE STORY TELLER, 1971
A GIFT FOR THE CHILDREN, 1973
MRS. STARLING'S PROBLEM, 1973

Contents

The Woman Who Was Changed

I

Eleanor Dane stood back to look at the dining table set for two. Her colored maid watched her with curiosity.

"I says when I was a-settin' it, ef I set 'em side by side they can both see the moon come up over the city."

Eleanor shook her head. Her lips quivered with a smile she would not allow. "Mattie, you sound so innocent, I can't believe you. You know perfectly well why you put us side by side. Moon over the city! I don't mind sitting by Kurt— but it's no good, Mattie. Save your strength!" She let herself smile now very steadily at Mattie. "I've been burned, Mattie! I'm staying away from the fire forever, now."

"Oh, goo'ness, Miss Eleanor!" Mattie wailed. "You make me tired. I jes' git so tired I feel like dyin'!" She flounced out of the door, swishing the towel with which she had been polishing the thick Swedish glass tumblers.

Eleanor Dane let the steady smile stay upon her lips. She looked at the two places, side by side. Then she changed one of them quickly to the end of the small rectangular table. She would sit at the head of her own table and Kurt would sit at her right. As for the moon—

The doorbell rang with a swift loud sharp note. That was Kurt. He always gave one hard deep push. His ring was never like anyone else's though, truly, she had very few with which to compare it. Everyone knew her name and almost no one knew her and almost no one came to her door. She thought of a letter she had received this morning from a young writer. "I hesitate," the girl had said, "to intrude upon your busy and brilliant life." She was busy enough—but what was a brilliant life? She lived alone. "I'm very happy," she said to herself.

Mattie had opened the door. Mattie's voice was saying smoothly, "Miss Eleanor's waitin' for you, Mr. Stenson."

"Thank you," said Kurt's voice, deep and abrupt.

Eleanor, putting down the last spoon, came out of the small dining room.

"I wasn't exactly waiting," she said, looking up at Kurt with her usual look of grave gaiety. "As a matter of fact, I was just finishing the table." She caught the glint of Mattie's rolling eye. "Bring the cocktails, Mattie," she said.

"Yas'm," said Mattie indignantly, and left the room.

"Sit down, Kurt," she said.

But Kurt stood, tall and waiting. "Where will you sit, Eleanor?" He had his own way of saying her name, and she liked its new sound upon his lips.

"Why?" she asked.

"I don't know where I want to sit until you are seated."

That, she thought quickly, meant she must not sit upon the couch, where Kurt could sit beside her. She chose the deep blue armchair. Now he must sit alone on the couch, away from her. He looked down at her, sunk in the deep chair.

"So," he said. He bent forward and put his hands upon the arms of the chair and pulled it closer to the couch. "So!" he said again.

She smiled, bracing herself against him.

"Now," he said, "I will—"

"Dinner will be ready in fifteen minutes," she broke in upon him. "No use saying, 'Now!' "

"Fifteen minutes is enough for me," he said. "It will also leave me time enough to say it all over again after dinner!"

"Oh, Kurt!" she cried. "Don't!"

"Eleanor, I will," he said. "I cannot be stopped. For the sixth time, on this third anniversary of the day I met you, will you marry me?"

Eleanor held herself away from him, braced delicately, poised, aloof, alone, smiling brightly. "No, Kurt."

"Still?" He stared at her, his piercing blue eyes, given him by his sea-faring Scandinavian ancestors, fixed upon her gray eyes.

"Still no!" she said clearly. "Kurt, forever *no!*"

"Not forever," he said, getting up abruptly. "Only until after dinner. I'm hungry. You, too, are hungry. After dinner we will feel better. Let us dine."

She did not answer. She rose and walked beside him across the room. She had been deciding, she was now almost decided, that after dinner she would say to Kurt very firmly and kindly that he must choose between two women, the woman she was now, or the woman she would be if she became his wife. If he chose that woman, his wife, then he must give her up altogether. For she had chosen. She had chosen to be what she was, herself, Eleanor Dane, novelist and writer. She would be no one else—not after those impossible years with Hartley.

"Kurt, will you sit here, at my right?" she said calmly. The little dining room looked perfect tonight, candles and silver, a white cloth, the doors open to the terrace, Mattie in black and white, waiting.

"Miss Eleanor"— Mattie's voice was like bottled honey—"I

done put you and Mr. Kurt side by side tonight, so you kin
see de moon rise."

Kurt's pleased voice broke in. "That's much better, Mattie!
Good Mattie!"

Mattie's eyes met Eleanor's, triumphant. "I knowed you
liked the moon, suh."

For a moment Eleanor was angry. Then she smiled. "Shall
we sit down, then, Kurt?" she said. Not even Mattie should
prevail.

No, nor the moon. When Mattie had brought in the salad,
she whispered, "Look, Miss Eleanor!" They looked. Among
the towers a glow was spreading like the prelude to music.
"It's the moon!"

"Is it, Mattie! You're so sentimental. Kurt, do you want
oil dressing?"

"Hush," said Kurt. "Wait!" He put his hand over hers on
the table.

She sat, bracing herself against them all. The glow deep-
ened. A strip of gold edged above a roof and grew wide and
round. In a minute it was glorious, full, swinging among the
towers. She pulled her hand away. But Kurt did not seem
to notice.

"I've seen it swing up like that," he said, "over the southern
seas, over the northern snows. Whenever I see it my spirit
leaps."

"Now will you have salad dressing, Kurt?" she said. The
moon! The moon had done her enough damage in her time.

"So, again, you will not marry me," said Kurt after dinner.

She had turned on all the lights against the moon. She had
no soft shaded lamps in her modern room. Light poured down
from metallic tubes, without glitter, without shadows. When
she had left Hartley's house three years ago, she had wanted
something utterly different from that old pillared house in
Virginia. New York, modern—

"So, again, I will not marry you," she said.

"I can't understand it," Kurt said. He was not hurt. He was too big for any hurt. He was simply puzzled. "You no longer care for that man who was your husband."

"I care no more for Hartley," she said quietly.

"You are sure?" Kurt's eyebrows shot up at her.

"Quite," she replied. "Besides, he's married again, very happily."

"That would not keep you from loving him," Kurt said quickly.

"But I do not," she said. "I am very happy."

"That's my enemy," he declared suddenly. "Your happiness! If I could only make you a little unhappy!"

"No one could make me unhappy," she replied.

"No? Eleanor, if I never came back, would you not be unhappy at all?"

"I should be very sorry," she said.

"Lonely?"

"And lonely," she said.

"But you don't love me?"

She hesitated, essentially truthful. If she had not been so truthful, she would never have had to leave Hartley.

"Part of me loves you," she said.

He laughed, a great free laugh, the laughter of a man used to being alone in space. "Now!" he cried. "Now we get somewhere!" He seized her hand.

"But only part," she said firmly. She let him have her hand for a moment. She was sure of herself. She was not afraid. She smiled, allowing the warmth to well for a moment from her heart. "How could I keep from loving you, indeed, Kurt? You give me such devotion. I know your heart. I am not a girl any more. I know how to value what you give me, though I cannot take it. It is the most precious thing in my life except the one thing which is my life."

"Your career!" He smiled a little sadly.

"No," she said quietly. "I don't care for a career. My work. That is different."

He sighed, looked at her hand for a moment, and then put it back upon her knee.

"Yes," he said, "it's different."

They sat quietly for a moment. She looked at him, and he looked down. She looked at him, at his rugged face and tossed fair hair. He was big, too big for his evening clothes, too big for her room. He fitted into another world than hers. If she took him into her world he would fill it, smash it, sweep her out of it. And into his world she would not go. She had had enough of trying to live in another's world. Her life was now what she wanted it to be. She was doing her work, hard and well, book after book.

"You will never believe it, that when we marry you shall do your work and I will do mine," he said.

"I know you would mean it to be so," she said. "I know it would not be possible."

"Then you do not know me. You are judging me, shaping me, thinking of me as a man like the man you knew."

"I've known other men," she said with the smallest smile.

"You do not know me!" he cried.

"Do I not, Kurt?"

"No!"

"Ah, let's talk of something else, shall we? This is finished."

"It is not finished, Eleanor, so long as I am alive."

"Kurt—"

"I am going. I want to go away. I want to think of what to do to show you myself."

"Dear Kurt—"

"No. I am going."

He went out, leaving the small perfect room empty and too still. She stood, looking at the front door. Then she turned and put out all the lights and drew back the blue curtains. Let the moonlight stream in. She need not be afraid of it now. She was alone—and safe.

In the moonlight she sat alone. But then, she wanted to be alone. On the night when she had left her home—Hartley's house—the little terrier had run after her to the car. For a moment she thought she would let it leap in beside her. It would be someone to be with her. But she did not. Even then she knew she must be alone. She would never dare to live with anything, anybody, again. She would not let herself be fond of any creature. For she would have said that Hartley, of all men, would have—

She had known him as long as she could remember. Hartley's father owned the bank in Richedale, and her father was editor of the newspaper. They went to Miss Boyne's dancing class. That, perhaps, was the first. Yes, that day Hartley came in wearing a new English suit with a round Eton collar, his straight dark hair brushed back. That was the first Hartley she knew. She stared at him with such abandon that, as he looked about the semicircle of little girls, her eyes caught him. He bowed to her unwillingly, a stiff little ducking bow, and she caught up her short skirts and danced out to meet him, laughing. She would not forget, no, nor could she ever forget, the displeasure on his face when he saw her laughing.

"What are you laughing for?" he demanded coldly. He could be cold, though he was only eleven. When other boys grew hot and red and doubled their fists Hartley grew cold and quiet and his dark gray eyes turned black.

"Why—for nothing!" she cried. Her heart, which had been running ahead of her happily, halted, dismayed.

"All right, then," he said. And without another word he led her out, his head very high above the stiff white collar. She had enjoyed the dance, half frightened while she did. Or had she enjoyed it because all the other little girls envied her his dark and lordly beauty?

He was always beautiful. When he was sixteen he was the valedictorian of their class in high school. Together they worked to make his speech the best that had ever been given. How they quarreled! For she had already the graceful casual style which later was to be her tool. And he did not like it.

"It makes everything sound as though it didn't matter," he complained.

"Oh, no, Hartley!" she urged. "Don't you see? Say it just this side of what you mean and it makes people laugh and wonder!"

"I'd rather say it my own way," he said proudly.

She had to learn even then that if she were to prevail with Hartley it must be without telling him. And this was not hard to do, because with all his cleverness he easily believed that he had done a thing alone. What she gave he took unaware, unless he disliked it. Only dislike could make him recognize what was not his own. It was fun at first, because she admired him so much, a creature both brilliant and beautiful. If she had been more than he, she might have given as eagerly, but not with laughter and loving amusement. But he needed nothing of her, in reality. He was so able for everything. It was the best valedictory they had ever had. Mr. Potkin, the principal, said so, over and over. She sat worshiping Hartley while Mr. Potkin, wiping his bald head, kept stammering to the audience, "Without casting discredit on previous efforts, I must say—I must say that in all my experience I have never heard—"

"It was your own speech, too, Hartley," she said to him after it was all over and they were driving home together in his new car. His father had given it to him that day.

"Of course it was mine!" he said calmly, his profile clear in the darkness.

She smiled, loving him. Her bits in it, she thought to herself, were her gift to him. It didn't matter if he didn't know she had given him anything. It was lovely to give and give, loving him.

Well, but perhaps that had started her long habit of secrecy. How much ought two people, loving each other, to try to share their life and thought? She used to puzzle over it even when she was at college in Bryn Mawr and Hartley was in Princeton. Her heart had said, "Everything!" All those years she wanted to share everything with Hartley. She poured out upon him all her thought and feelings. If she went out with another man she must tell him how it happened, where she went, how she felt. And he wrote back, telling her in meticulous closeness of his own life. When they met at vacations they began at once, knowing everything between.

"Isn't our love perfect?" she had demanded of him joyously.

"Perfect!" he had declared.

. . . It was a hard habit to break, that habit of sharing all one's life. When Kurt came to see her now, sometimes when they were alone together in this room into which Hartley would never come, she had a curious feeling of guilt, a compulsion to tell, to tell—it was to tell Hartley. She ought not to be seeing Kurt unless Hartley knew, her heart's habit said. She smiled in the moonlight, got up and fumbled for a cigarette, lit it, and sat down again.

Hartley was married to Elsa Freed.

The moon was above the windows now, so there was only the light upon the floor. Her slippered feet were bathed in it. She could imagine warmth, the light lay so brightly about her feet. But of course moonlight was cold.

. . . When had she first begun to live by herself? She had begun bit by bit. She pinched off a moment here, an hour there, not knowing she was doing it. She and Hartley had married the summer they were graduated from college. For why should they wait? they asked themselves. He was going into the bank with his father. All the parents were pleased.

"It's all so perfect, darling Eleanor!" Hartley's mother kept saying. She was tall and a little too big, but her features that were so exactly Hartley's were still fine and unchanged. Hartley would not look different however long he lived, and when he lay dead his straight profile, his clearly shaped lips would not be changed. His mother had the same lips, clean and sweet in the way they folded. But they were firm.

"It's so ideal!" she kept saying to Eleanor. "If you knew how mothers worry about their sons! But I haven't worried about Hartley. His love for you has been his anchor."

She was good, too—Hartley's mother. She was not in the

least jealous or possessive, though Hartley was her only child. Eleanor had loved her. It was sad, since she was going to die last year, that she had not died a little earlier and never known about the divorce. It was such a grief to her.

"I can't *understand* it, darlings!" she had kept crying, her still lovely lips trembling and the tears rolling down her creamy old cheeks. "I don't see what's the matter!"

Eleanor said at last, very gently, "Mother, Hartley doesn't love the woman I've grown to be—the woman that is really me."

But this only bewildered her. "Why, Eleanor, he's loved you all these years!"

Eleanor, shaking her head, had written to Hartley, "You tell her, Hartley! Tell her anything you like. I can't make her understand."

So Hartley had gone alone and tried to tell her. "Mother, Eleanor cares more for her work than she does for me."

"Why, Hartley, how can you say such things? Eleanor has loved only you for years!"

And she cried for Eleanor to be brought to her and she besought both of them, "Darlings, you're both mistaken. You each think the other one has stopped loving. I know you haven't. Dears, turn and tell each other, here before your old mother! Oh, Hartley, your beautiful home! Eleanor's made a beautiful home! Eleanor, he's been so proud of you!"

But Hartley said in a low voice, "She won't give up her work for me, Mother."

"Oh, Eleanor, if he doesn't want you to write— After all, a woman's real work is her house and—"

"But why should I have to give it up, Mother?" Eleanor stood very straight. Standing straight like this, she came just under Hartley's shoulder. It had been one of their little jokes. He would peer over his shoulder and call, "Still there?"

And she must answer, "Forever!"

"Oh, my darling!" Hartley's mother wailed. "To save your home, yourself, your husband!"

She had shaken her head and whispered, trembling, but blindly sure, "I can't save myself that way—and if I don't save myself, nothing is saved."

. . . She was trembling even now, sitting here with her feet in the moonlight, alone, that old trembling. But she was still sure. She would have been lost if she had given it up.

For what Hartley could never see was that she didn't care at all about the success. It was pleasant, of course. How could she help being pleased when letters began pouring in on her, telling her what a wonderful thing she had done in writing *Storm Tonight*? What did the money mean, the praise, the uproar of newspaper reporters and publicity? She had genuinely hated it, but Hartley could not believe she did.

"If you really hated it," he kept saying, "you'd give up writing."

"I can't," she said. They were in the lovely old living room. That was the day when the reporters from New York had come.

"Aren't you coming to New York?" they had demanded. "You can't stay in a little place like Richedale now—why, all New York wants to see you—to hear you—"

She had looked at Hartley as they sat side by side on the couch.

"This is my home," she said. "I can't leave my home." She put her hand quickly in Hartley's. But he did not move.

"Aren't you very proud of your famous wife, Mr. Bainbridge?" a silly girl reporter asked.

"I've always been proud of her," Hartley said clearly.

"But now," the girl persisted, "now you must be—oh, just bursting!"

Hartley only smiled. He had a charming smile when he turned to give it fully. The girl smiled back at him. She began to scribble hastily.

But it had been a relief to see them all go, to open the windows after them. "I want to clear the very smell of them out," she said gaily. And that was the night she had the maid serve dinner by the fire. She had drawn the old gold velvet curtains and lit the fire, though the Southern October was not cold.

"Home's so sweet," she kept saying. Just beyond these walls there were crowds waiting. She had somehow given them something of herself and they liked it. They wanted more of her, all of her. They wanted her to lecture, to show herself. She was afraid of them, of importunate women in clubs, of strange eager men wanting to drag her out of her home. But she had drawn the curtains and she was safe here in her house with her husband. She was very happy. She wanted nothing changed, forever. In her contentment she began to laugh.

"Weren't they a funny lot of people this afternoon, dearest?" she cried. "Think of making your living going from one celebrity to another! Isn't it silly, darling, *me* being a celebrity?"

She looked at him, expecting his laughter. But he did not laugh. Instead he said with the coldness which always frightened her, "You like it, I think, Eleanor."

"Oh, no, Hartley," she cried, protesting. "Oh, no! I hate it, truly I do!"

So he said, "If you really hated it, you'd give it up."

And so she said, "I can't."

That was the first time.

Searching, searching the past now in this new present, so that she might know how to shape her future, she saw it was at that moment she had been born again. A small struggling independent human soul had been born in her woman's body which had so long belonged to Hartley. That soul was herself, her own. All the years of her youth and her young womanhood she had been Hartley's, and her own soul had lain sleeping. It had not even occurred to her that it was not his right to command her life and time because she loved him. In the morning she planned the day about him. What time he did not want her she took for her own.

"Shall you be home for lunch, Hartley?"

"No, I have a business luncheon today."

"Then I'll have lunch with Myra."

"All right."

And scarcely knowing it, she had come to let him shape her beliefs and thoughts.

"Hartley, what do you really think about Communism?"

"I think it's dangerous nonsense, darling. People who are making a success of their lives aren't Communists. It's only the unsuccessful."

"Perhaps they're the frightened," she had said, imagining them. "Perhaps they need to feel themselves tied to other people."

"Ah, perhaps," he had said and smiled. "You've always to take on yourself the burdens of the world, haven't you, little Nora?"

It was true she was always thinking about people, imagining how they felt. Mrs. Battie, for instance, the laundress—how did it feel to spend your life going from one basement to another, living in steam and suds? She sat on the cellar steps, talking to Mrs. Battie.

"Have you children, Mrs. Battie?"

"Two boys, ma'am. I wish they'd been girls. Girls stay by you. But Denny's in jail and Tom's a tramp. He was a tramp from the day he took his first step. Born to run away, he was. Lickin' 'im was no good."

"Why is Denny in jail, Mrs. Battie?"

"I dunno exactly, honey. The judge put 'im in and I guess he know what he put 'im in for. I took 'is word for it."

"Why, it's dreadful!" she cried.

Mrs. Battie wrung out a dripping sheet. "It ain't bad at all, dearie. You know where they are, in jail, and you know they got food and clothes. I wish I knew Tom was in a good jail somewheres."

"And Mr. Battie?" she breathed. She was ashamed of her endless curiosity, but she had to know about people—everybody, everywhere.

"He's passed on, dearie. He drunk himself into a decline years ago."

She went away to brood over Mrs. Battie.

"Mrs. Battie's all alone," she told Hartley. "Her husband's dead, and her sons—"

"Why do you care about such people?" Hartley said with irritation.

"I don't know," she said humbly. Nobody else did. Other women like herself said, "Good morning, Mrs. Battie. You'll find the soap and everything ready," and forgot her.

After a while Eleanor had written a story about Mrs. Battie and when it was published she read it with painful eagerness. Yes, it was right. There was Mrs. Battie, set out in black and white, not the Mrs. Battie in the basement, but a living woman shaped from Mrs. Battie's clay. Only then could she forget her. But by that time there would be someone else. And these people, these shapings, were the separate life she began to have, the life away from Hartley.

And she said to Hartley, "I can't give it up."

For she knew she could not. Yes, it was like a drug, that necessity, that urgency to keep on creating people, action, life. She had begun it soon after her marriage, in bits, at her desk, and the bits had taken on life and form. It had begun out of a sort of emptiness she did not understand. For surely her life was very full. Richedale was a pleasant little city with more rich people in it than poor. And young Mrs. Hartley Bainbridge was invited everywhere. But it had not been quite enough. She went everywhere—and loved to go. She loved people anywhere—not only people like Mrs. Battie. She wanted to hear them all talk, to see how they all moved and walked, to watch them feel. And at first she came home and told everything to Hartley. Long Sunday afternoons when they drove into the country she would tell him bits of things that came up in her mind. Sunday mornings, of course, they went to church.

"Dearest, I've been trying for weeks to think—of course,

it's a penguin that Mrs. Brace looks like—a penguin, of course! I couldn't think until this morning she came into church in that stiff black satin with the white vest, and I saw it at once—you know, the little black satin toque. I've felt so relieved, now that I know!"

Hartley shouted with laughter. "Eleanor, you idiot!"

"But she *is* a penguin!" she protested.

And then when she got home she couldn't forget it, and while Hartley sat reading Santayana that night—he loved Santayana and she didn't—she wrote down something about Mrs. Brace and laughed.

"Listen, Hartley!" she cried. She read it aloud and he listened. Then he laughed, too.

"You've made her," he said.

Well, later Mrs. Brace had made *Storm Tonight.* That's what had made the book sell, her old funny shape waddling through the pages like a fussy fairy godmother. Hundreds of letters said that. They said over and over again, "I've *known* your old penguin lady, bless her! She reminds me of—"'

How it had begun she scarcely knew. But she let Mrs. Brace grow and grow into hundreds of pages. Mrs. Brace had taken her away from Hartley.

. . . She rose, and, standing at the window of her modern room in New York City, she stared down into the people. Perhaps it had begun because when she and Hartley were married she had not needed to write letters any more. She missed that writing. Every day she had crystallized into words the life that she saw. She thought it had been to share with him. But perhaps even then her gift was stirring in her. Now, remembering, she realized that often she had forgotten Hartley. She had sat for hours writing, changing, making people come to life. And in the end it had grown to mean more than anything. So might God have sat, idling with clay, to find in terror Adam, a living creature he had made. And Adam and his seed took the whole earth away from God in the end. There they were, running to and fro. She pulled up a chair and sat watching the cars, at this height seeming to slide up and down the bright street. People, people! She was deathlessly curious about them, afraid of them, lonely without them, and lonely with them. . . .

Yes, she had been lonely even with Hartley. For why otherwise had she kept on with her eternal writing even when at last she knew it would cost her everything? One day he would say, "You will have to choose between your writing and me."

How silly of me, she had thought when that idea first sprang into her mind! As though Hartley would say such a dramatic thing! He was the least dramatic of men, the least demanding, really. He was a wonderful husband.

Myra said to her often, "You don't know how lucky you are, Nora! Hartley's a rock. Nobody could get him away from you. He's so in love with you I don't believe it occurs to him to know another woman is alive, though he's so good-looking! I wish I were half as sure of my Hal!"

She had smiled at Myra without answering. She had been sorry for her. Everybody knew how Hal acted over young girls. But today Myra and Hal were still together—and Hartley was married to Elsa Freed. Strange, strange! And Myra was so strong and independent and could have lived alone so much more easily than she. But she had learned how to do it at last. You could learn how to do anything.

. . . It was growing late. The after-theater taxis were whizzing up the street and the downtown traffic was slackening. Past her door she heard footsteps and laughing voices. But her own rooms were still. For a moment she wished she had her little dog. Then she thought resolutely, "No, I'm not going to get to be a woman with a dog—not at thirty-two." She rose and snapped on the tubular lights and poured herself a small glass of sherry and sipped it, and ate a dry cracker. Then she picked up a crumb, emptied the ash tray, took the glass into the kitchen, and went into her own room.

. . . It was at night, going to bed, that she was most alone.

She was so used to someone splashing in the shower, whistling. Hartley had a clear hard whistle that was full of music. He'd made a trick of it and he could whistle long intricate melodies, things like the airs from *Tannhäuser* and Beethoven. And then he came in, his wet hair shining and black. They'd had a lot of fun.

Sometimes now she wondered how she had ever given up the sheer fun of living with someone as charming as Hartley. He had been so gay. When they were first married he used to run home from the bank and leap up the steps and shout for her. And she always heard his footsteps and was there. How they laughed over nothing! The old house, for instance— his mother had insisted on their having her own old house. It had belonged to her father, had been sold, and she had bought it back for them. It was too big, but she said they were to fill it with children. While they waited for the children they laughed at the high ceilings, the huge square rooms.

"We'll have to have hundreds of children," she laughed to Hartley. And when she eyed a corner and said, "Don't you think that side of the room looks bare, darling?" he would say cautiously, "We'll have to set a child there." But no children had come—not in ten years of their marriage. After a while they stopped talking about them, and then when she was writing she forgot to miss them or to mind that they would never come. Still, if she'd had children— Well, even if she'd had children, there was her own soul.

She climbed into the low wide bed where she had lain alone for these three years. A new book lay on the glass-topped table beside her, and she picked it up. She would read for a while and put the years out of her mind. For her life was now broken off clean. This was herself, living. But she could not read. The old pondering questions were written more blackly on the pages than another's story.

. . . And how had it begun that Hartley had told her she must make her choice? For at first he had been amused at her stories. She read them aloud to him in the evenings, eager for his praise, his judgment. And he was generous with praise.

"Do you *see* him, darling, as I write him down?" she pressed him.

"It's a perfect picture," he said, laughing. "Why, I see him and hear him!"

Later no praise of great critics had been so sweet. "Greatest novel of our times" . . . "Epic sweep of character" . . . none of it had been so precious. Once he had said, his face grave, his eyes strange, "I believe you've something—more than we know, perhaps." What was the look in his eyes? It—she had imagined it—was hostile, almost hostile. She had thrown herself into his arms. "Oh, no," she had said. "I'm nothing—it's nothing. I only amuse myself—it's my kind of play. I get so bored at bridge." She had drawn his arms about her. "I'm only your wife, darling, darling!"

And he had held her and said, "Of course, dear heart!" And fear had passed away from her.

But that morning when the telegram had come announcing the award of the prize to *Storm Tonight,* there was the look again. She had put on her hat and walked down the street to the bank to find him. No one should know until he did. She thought for a moment of her parents, dead and unknowing. But Hartley was alive. She had him to tell.

She went straight to his office, smiling, seeing no one, her feet electric with joy. She opened the door. He was dictating to Miss Reese.

"Just a moment, Eleanor," he said. And she sat down, waiting. She was always a little afraid of him here in the bank. His father had died a year ago and, young as he was, he had been appointed to his father's place. He was a man to be trusted. He sat dictating carefully.

"We regret very much that we are unable to make the loan, but upon the report of our committee, the security you offer seems inadequate."

The telegram burned in her hand. She smiled, her eyes dancing, watching him. But he did not look at her. He was very punctilious in the office.

"Yours—and so forth. That's all, Miss Reese."

"Yes, sir."

He waited until his plain-looking secretary had closed the door softly. Then he said, "Well, Eleanor?"

She came to him and held out the yellow slip without a word. He took it and read it. She stood beside him, waiting, her heart pounding.

Then he looked up. And there in his eyes was that hostility. She was terrified by it. She tore the telegram from his hands and dropped to her knees and hid her face against him.

"I don't care about it," she said, strangled. "Don't—don't look at me like that!"

"Why, why—" he said. "Get up, my dear. Someone might come in."

But she clung to him.

"I'm your wife," she whispered.

"Of course you are," he said again, and he forced her gently away from him. "And I'm very proud of you, and it's fine news—why, it's just splendid, of course. Let's see—what is it? A thousand dollars, isn't it?"

"It's not the money." She was sobbing now. "It's—it's an honor."

"Of course it is," he said heartily. He was patting her hand. "Didn't I say I was proud of you?—Now stop crying, Nora. What made you start crying anyway? We'll talk about it at dinner tonight. I want to hear all about it."

"Aren't you coming home to lunch?" she asked, dismayed.

"No, I was about to call you up. We have to have a directors' meeting." He took up the telephone. "Miss Reese?"

Her little newborn soul suddenly reared to its feet. She wiped her eyes, straightened her hat, and bent and kissed the top of his head.

"Goodbye then, dearest," she said.

"Goodbye, my love," he said. "Yes, please, Miss Reese. I forgot one point in that last letter—"

She started and then stopped. She stooped and picked up

the crumpled telegram. She might want it. And, after all, it was hers. He did not notice it.

That night he said, "Well, it's splendid news, Eleanor. Yes indeed."

And she smiled. "Yes, isn't it?" And then she said, "Shall we go over to Myra's after dinner?" and he said, "I think it would be pleasant, dear."

And all evening she listened to hear if he shouted, "Do you know what Eleanor's done?"

But he did not, and she said nothing. It didn't matter, she told herself. Tomorrow it would be in all the papers and they would all know. Tomorrow Myra would rush over and shake her and scream, "When did you know, you monkey?"

"Last night."

"You and Hartley both knew last night and you never said one word?"

She'd just smile. It didn't matter.

. . . Here in this room alone it mattered horribly. She got up and opened a drawer and took out a scrapbook. There the telegram was, pasted against a page. She had it still.

She climbed back into bed and covered herself neatly, and lay very straight and still. . . .

At first it had been such fun. She had had praise enough in her time, for she had been a pretty girl and had grown into a pretty woman. It had come to be a matter of course that people said, "How lovely you are in that blue!" Hartley said over and over, "I'm glad I have a beautiful wife." And she was glad she was pretty because he would have minded it if she had not been. But she had never been vain. Her mother had seen to that. "Only silly women are vain, Eleanor," her strong mother had said. "Use your good looks as an asset, not a weakness." Besides, she secretly did not consider herself beautiful. She liked decided coloring, fair or dark, and she was neither. Her eyes were gray and her hair a tawny brown, and her nose was not quite straight enough. She loved the straight clarity of Hartley's profile, disliking her own irregularity. People talked of the changefulness of her face, but that she could not see.

And so when praise was heaped upon her, when she heard such huge words as "a dramatic new talent," "genius," she still was not vain. She laughed inside herself, thinking, "It's only me!" Her stories—they were only old Mrs. Brace and Mrs. Battie and Sam, the furnace man, and Mr. Black who had the drugstore, and such people. That could not be genius.

Still, perhaps she had been a little vain without knowing it. Else why would she have been so bewildered and so hurt when Hartley began to find fault with her? She had lived with him in a sort of quiet gaiety for years. She knew, of course, that he was not quite what she had imagined him at their wedding day. Then it had seemed unbelievable, yet true, that he had not a single fault. In his arms, when they woke for the first time together, she said with a sort of awe, "There is not one thing in you that I would change if I could!" And he smiled and said nothing, since, indeed, there was nothing to say. He had high standards, but he too believed that he fulfilled them.

She came to see after a while that, though he did achieve them, still he could only do so if everything about him was as he liked it. She did not see this for a long time. At first she was continually doing small things which brought coldness to his eyes. She was not punctual. She could sit writing and forget everything. At last she would become aware of something inside herself tearing at her attention. When she forced herself to see what it was, it was the clock's face staring at her. She had put it in front of her. Hartley had said, "Meet me at one o'clock." They were lunching together. He still said, "I'd rather lunch with you than anyone alive. It's a bright spot in the day." But if she did not meet him at one, he would greet her coldly. "I've been waiting—" he would say in exact minutes. So she learned to heed time. There was no story so powerful in her that even deeper was not Hartley's command, "Meet me at one." She learned to dress in a flash of flying feet and snatching hands, so that before she met him she counted ten to stop her panting. Yes, that cold look in his eyes grew to be her conscience.

Still, it was very easy, when she loved him so well, to keep his life smooth so that he could be the sort of man he wanted to be. It meant only to see that he had what he liked to eat, that his home was quiet and beautiful, that when he came home his fresh garments lay ready for him to change, and that she was there waiting. . . . It was a strange thing, she thought now, in her bed, with all time her own, how those hours when he was away had folded into no time at all. Actually, she had had hours to herself. She wrote for hours every day. But they seemed nothing at all. Over them hung the inexorableness of the moment when she must stop, regardless of what crisis her people were in. Yes, that was one of her new freedoms. Now in the morning she began with her people and went with them until of their own will they let her go. She had said to Mattie, "Never come near me when I am in my study. Don't come and tell me dinner or lunch or anything is ready. The important thing is, when *I'm* ready." She had run her life by meals for years. Her books were checkerboarded with meals. Sometimes, reading them, she was dissatisfied. There was a break, a drop in the long mounting movement. "It must have been I had to stop there for dinner," she thought. It seemed impossible to her now that her life had once been ordered, her work marred, by such small circumstances.

Yet at the time it had not occurred to her that it was a hardship. That life of her own, struggling upward through her work, had learned, like a tree deprived of air and sun, to shape itself to what had then seemed necessity. She would never have known it was hardship if Hartley had not suddenly begun to find fault with her.

"I don't want to hurt you, my darling," he had said gently one evening—it was a November evening, by the fire—"but I wonder if you realize that you raise your voice now when you speak?"

"Do I?" she exclaimed. "Oh, I am so sorry! I didn't know I did."

"Of course you didn't," he said. "That's why I spoke of it. But ever since you have been speaking in public, I have noticed it."

It was true that in a shy tentative fashion she had been speaking here and there in nearby towns. The women in the clubs were so proud of her and they gave her luncheons which it seemed ungracious not to accept. And they always wanted her to talk about how she had come to write. They poured eager questions upon her. "Do you find your having a profession interferes with your home life?" they asked again and again. And she always laughed and said, "It might, if I didn't have a perfect husband!" She was always grateful to Hartley in those days that he let her write. It was much later that the question came up in her heart like a blast of dynamite. "Why should I be grateful to him for letting me be myself?"

So now she said to him, "I'll try to think of it and keep my voice low. Thank you for telling me, darling."

And he said "Your soft voice has been one of the things I've loved most in you."

She smiled at him warmly. "I want to be what you want me to be," she said.

"You are," he replied, "or I wouldn't have taken you to be my wife."

And they went on with their evening. Still, now she realized it was not quite the same, although she would not have said so then.

For she had come to doubt after a while that she was quite what he wanted, and the doubt began that evening. It took a long time, because they were so close. She had grown so into his life that without knowing it she had become completely dependent on him for everything. To know that one day she would live alone like this would have terrified her. She had never spent the night alone. She dared not drive the car through traffic. He talked to tradesmen, and he arranged their travel every winter. She was sheltered until she was helpless and she did not know it. As her work grew to take on a life of its own she grew with it, still not knowing she did. For she never had thought much about herself. Her mother had been a domineering brilliant woman, demanding much of her only child, and Eleanor had yielded to her. To yield to Hartley was only an extension of childhood habit.

Then there was the day her publisher came all the way from New York to see her.

Hartley said, "This is one of my very busy days. I shan't be able to take any time away from the bank, not even for lunch."

"Oh, it won't be necessary," she said quickly. "He will only call and go away."

But he did not. She found herself talking with him eagerly and fully about her next book. It was such pleasure to talk about her work to someone who listened attentively and with supreme interest. She felt suddenly free and very happy. When at last everything was said, she leaned back in her chair and laughed.

"I'm ashamed! I haven't talked like that in my life!"

And he answered gravely, "I know now you are a great writer, because you have so much in yourself. I am proud to publish your books. Goodbye." He stood up to go, a tall pleasant middle-aged figure, and hesitated. "Unless you— Are you free to lunch with me?"

She liked him so much, it was so warming to find someone who knew what she meant, that she answered ardently, "I'm alone—my husband can't come home today. I'd like it more than anything." And so, forgetting she didn't drive well in traffic, she drove the car through the streets to a country inn and afterward to his train.

She enjoyed it so much. She even drove a little while alone, smiling to herself. She was, she thought, such a fortunate woman. She had so much—Hartley, home, friends. And now coming to her was success in her work. She felt it coming as she might feel the throbbing of distant approaching drums.

She reached home in the late spring afternoon, dreamy with happiness.

When she entered the house the mood dropped from her like a silver cloak.

"What have I been doing!" she thought in guilt. "I've forgotten everything. I didn't even remember to ask Hartley when he was coming home!"

She flew upstairs, calling softly, "Darling! Darling!" But no one answered. She went downstairs to the kitchen to ask Hester, the maid, "Has there been any message from Mr. Bainbridge?"

"No'm, not a word," Hester replied. She was shelling peas. "Want I should make a cold or hot dessert?" she asked.

Eleanor pondered. It was always difficult to think of things to eat. Hartley liked variety.

"What did we have last night?" she asked.

"You had lemon tart," Hester said. "Want I should make a chocolate puddin'?"

"It's warm tonight," Eleanor said anxiously. "Let's have something cold—a fruit jelly with whipped cream."

"If it were I," she thought idly, going upstairs to bathe and put on a fresh gown, "I'd never think again what to eat. I'd eat anything rather than think about it."

. . . She did not dream then that one day she would really never think about it. She said to Mattie, "Never ask me what to eat. If you ever do, I'll eat nothing." Even when Kurt came to dinner she never said, "Have roast beef because Mr. Stenson likes it." . . .

But then, going up the stairs, she forgot her wish. She forgot it while she brushed her hair until it gleamed and while she put on the deep blue gown of chiffon that Hartley liked. She was just putting its silver rose into place when she heard his footstep in the hall, and she ran out and stood at the head of the stairs, smiling.

He came up the stairs slowly, gazing at her. "You've been waiting for me," he said.

"No," she said gaily. "I'm only just back. I've been out!"
He paused three steps away.

"Where?" he asked.

"We went out to lunch!" she cried. "And I drove the car to the Blue Swan myself, and afterward to the station. I didn't have any trouble at all, darling."

"That didn't take all afternoon," he said, and came no nearer.

"I took a little drive," she said coaxingly. She put out her arms and touched his shoulders.

"By yourself?" he asked, unbelieving.

"All by myself," she said. She was a little afraid now. Were his eyes growing cold? She came down a step, two steps, three, and stood beside him and leaned against him.

"I came home safely," she said, and whispered, "Don't scold me!"

He put his arms around her and kissed the top of her head. "I never scold," he said. He kissed her again. "Only don't forget I don't like damned independent women."

"I'm not independent, really," she besought him.

"No, of course not," he said. "Now I must rest a bit. God, what a day I've had!"

"Oh, darling," she cried quickly, "I've been keeping you!" She flew ahead of him to draw his bath and put out his clothes. "Tell me about it!"

She sat in his room while he talked to her from the bathroom, splashing between sentences. "We had that whole business of the mortgages on the Staunton place to go into. It's fallen due and it looks as though the heirs were going to let the place go. . . ."

She listened on and on to his detailed day. After dinner, perhaps, she would tell him what her publisher had said.

But after dinner they had that strange quarrel that came up like an unexpected storm. They had never quarreled before. She had not dreamed of quarreling with Hartley. He was sitting on the couch and she, before she sat down, bent to kiss him, lightly, quickly, on the cheek.

"That's no kiss!" he said sharply. "That's a peck!"

"A butterfly kiss," she said. "It's only to begin with."

She kissed him again, for the first time in their life with self-consciousness. Consciously she pressed her lips to his in a long kiss.

"There," she said, drawing away to look at him. "Is that better?"

But he looked at her, the gathering coldness dark in his eyes.

"I've been feeling you changed," he said slowly. "For a long time I've been feeling you were growing different."

His coldness drove into her heart.

"Why, darling—why—why—" she stammered. She fumbled for his hand, but he began to light a cigarette.

"I hadn't meant to say anything," he said in a low voice. "In fact, I made up my mind I wouldn't. But it's got to a place where I can't bear it."

"Hartley!" she whispered. "What do you mean?"

"You don't seem to be here any more," he said. "Your mind is somewhere else. You—"

"But—but I am here, darling," she broke in. "What do I do that is different?"

He thought a moment, looking gravely at his cigarette ash, while she watched him anxiously.

"It isn't so much what you do as what you don't do," he said at last.

"What do I leave undone?" she asked.

"Little things—only little things."

At that moment she felt stirring her own new soul. It had grown during the afternoon, and during the drive alone. She said, almost angrily, "No, but—Hartley, I insist. You've said a dreadful thing. How am I different?"

He turned on her. "You're different this instant." He

mocked her. " 'I insist—I insist!' " His voice dropped. "That's not my Nora. That's another woman entirely."

She was staring at him. Out of some depth in her, her soul was struggling up to her lips to speak for her. In a moment it would be speaking. "May I not change, then? May I not grow and develop? Must I be at thirty the immature yielding creature I was at twenty?"

She was afraid of her soul, fighting toward her lips. But before it could reach its voice he seized her in his arms, pleading, "Darling, I love you—stay as you are!"

"I am the same," she said against his lips. Then she drew away. "No, but Hartley—let me speak! I am always the same. I can never change to you. It doesn't matter what comes to me of—of success—it can't change me to you!"

His arms dropped. "Yes, it must," he said. "It is changing you, and if you are changed, you are changed to me, too."

Her heart shivered. "Do you mean—you— You don't mean you can't love me?"

"Of course I don't mean anything so radical as that," he said impatiently. "I only mean—well, I married one woman and if she changes into another—you see? I have to adjust—if I can. I don't know this new woman."

She wet her dry lips. "Now, Hartley, I must know what you mean. This is my life or my death. I am conscious of nothing—"

"That's what makes it so—so irrevocable," he said. "It's instinct working in you. Instinct is much worse than effort."

"Tell me how—in what way—I've changed," she said, pressing him. "Give me chapter and verse."

"Well, here," he said abruptly. "I used to feel that you were entirely interested in me and my work. Now I feel you have a separate life and only part of you is interested in me and what I do."

She pondered this. "I see," she said slowly. "I can see how you would feel that."

"Even—even when we make love," he went on, "you don't

give yourself as you did. There's a part of you that doesn't join!"

"Hartley—oh, Hartley!" she said in a low voice.

"It's true," he maintained. "Do you think I don't know?" He hurried on. "I could endure that. But it stands to reason that all this coming and going of reporters and publishers and whatnot—all this stuff in the papers—" He paused.

"All this stuff—" she prompted him, half dazed.

He stirred impatiently and lit another cigarette. "It comes to this," he said irritably. "You're my wife. I want you to stay my wife."

"You mean—"

"I mean I won't have my wife's name—*my* name—all over the newspapers. And there's another thing I never told you. I didn't want to hurt you. But I don't like the things you write. *Storm Tonight*—there's good stuff in it—that old woman's funny, of course. But that scene between the man and the two girls—I don't want everybody thinking you know about such stuff as that. I don't want men thinking you must be some sort of a—loose woman to know such things. How *do* you know it, anyway?" He turned on her fiercely. "I've wanted to ask you that—I've thought of it in the night—how the devil does *she* know such things! I've asked myself. I've been ashamed to ask you."

She sat with burning heart and cold hands. "I don't know," she whispered. "Only that kind of a man—he would have acted like that!"

"And how'd you know such a man?" he retorted.

"I don't," she faltered. "I made him up."

"A nice filthy imagination!" he said.

And she said nothing at all. Her people, it was true, behaved as they would. When she was writing them down she wrote things she did not know and only felt. She couldn't help feeling. She couldn't help— "I can't help it," she said.

"Well, it comes to this," he said abruptly. "You've got to be my wife, or else not my wife."

The incredible words he spoke as clearly, as calmly as ever he spoke anything. She might have thought he felt nothing, except at that moment he stretched out his hand toward the ash tray and his hand was trembling.

"Darling!" she cried in a low voice. "Oh, my darling! This between us!"

But he would not turn to her tenderness.

"It's come to this pass between us," he repeated. "Will you be my wife, or will you not?"

. . . Beside her bed the telephone began to ring harshly into the still room. She dragged herself dazed out of the past and took up the receiver. Kurt shouted in her ear. His voice was a strong wind, sweeping away everything.

"Eleanor, Eleanor?"

"Yes, Kurt?"

"Eleanor, I am going to the Himalayas!"

"Kurt!"

"Yes! I have this moment a cable from Hardinger. He will finance this expedition. I shall find the blue flowers. I shall—" He paused suddenly. "My Eleanor! Tomorrow at nine o'clock I shall come to ask you to marry me."

She laughed. "No, you won't, Kurt Stenson! I work until one o'clock, and I see nobody—nobody, do you hear!"

"Then I come at one o'clock and I take you to lunch and after lunch I ask you to marry me!"

She laughed again. "Well, since I shan't see you for so long, I will have lunch with you once more!"

"What do you mean, not see me? You go with me on our honeymoon! Honeymoon in the Himalayas!"

She shook her head, laughing, and hung up the receiver.

II

In the bright sunshine which Kurt loved she looked across the table at him. He had stridden across the crowded hotel dining room ahead of the waiter to this window.

"I don't know why these New Yorkers like to eat in darkness," he had shouted as he went. "They like to eat in dungeons and cellars and holes in the ground! Come to the sun, Eleanor!" Around him people had looked up at him tolerantly and smiled.

"Here!" he had said in triumph and pushed aside the waiter and pulled out her chair. So she had sat down laughing and looked at him, the sunshine beating upon his thick fair hair and ruddy fair skin, plumbing his sea-blue eyes. It fell on her, too, perhaps with less mercy, she thought. But she did not care. She had no wish to entice Kurt. She was as she was.

"And now," Kurt had just said, "we have finished! And it is time for the next thing. Here is a cigarette you shall smoke to keep you calm while I propose marriage—no, I am wrong—no sedative! You are already too calm while I make love to you. I will give you champagne. Waiter!"

"Kurt!" she protested, laughing. "Don't be ridiculous!"

But he would not listen. His eyes were shining. He was laughing, too.

"Waiter! Champagne! Your best! Now then, my Eleanor!"

She watched the champagne bubbling out of the bottle into her glass, half embarrassed at the nonsense which held the discomfort of being half serious, too.

"Are you ready, Eleanor?" Kurt was leaning toward her, his glass in his hand. "To our honeymoon in the Himalayas!"

She shook her head. "I can't drink to that, Kurt!"

"No? Why not? It will be, you know."

"It will never be," she said quietly.

"I shall make it," he said firmly.

But she only shook her head again. "Not even you, dear Kurt."

He looked at her steadily a moment, his eyes not less shining because they were grave.

"At least drink to me, Eleanor, and I will drink to you."

"I will gladly, Kurt."

They drank.

"Now," said Kurt, "I will tell you about our honeymoon. I have the maps all ready."

He pulled out of his large coat pocket a bundle of maps and spread them over the table. His face was lighted with eagerness, his big slender hands quick. She sat, half smiling, gazing at the roads his finger outlined toward the Himalayas.

"Two ways, my Eleanor! First, across the Atlantic, we go to Sweden. For there is my small mother waiting to see you. She has been saying ever since I can remember, 'Kurt, why don't you bring me a daughter? I am tired of only three sons and not one daughter. You are the eldest and you should begin something.' And I will say, 'Mother, I have—here is your daughter.' You will like my small mother, Eleanor. She has such blue eyes and such red cheeks and her hair is so white. And she will live in the country only with her chickens and her cows. So! And then"—his finger moved swiftly south— "so across Germany and to Constantinople—so! And then south again and the Red Sea—and the long warm days and the warm moonlit nights and the warm seas about us, my darling—"

He lifted his eyes and she could not speak. It was no use to speak now. She would save everything for the last final refusal.

"And so, my darling, to India. And I shall not have you linger in India. It is a sad country—not for honeymoons. We will go north at once to the mountains, up to the sunshine and the snows. Then I shall gather my men and my horses. And I shall see that you have a cream-white pony, my Eleanor! I know an old man at a foothill town. He is half Tartar, and he breeds ponies for the mountains. I shall look at all his ponies until I find one beautiful to see, sure of foot, swift-spirited but careful of his burden. Then you and I will ride up and up into the mountains. We shall talk together of everything. I shall know you, and you know me, every moment of our lives since we were born. So our lives will become one."

She sat, listening. She could see the winding mountain roads, the cream-white pony, the mountains. There would be cold clear days, the silent starry nights.

He was saying, "And there, my darling, among the snows of the glacier, we will find our flowers blooming, you and I!"

It was yet another life. She had known two lives, the one with Hartley, the one she had now. She had been two women, the woman who was Hartley's wife, the woman who lived alone. But the woman Kurt was telling her about, the woman riding the cream-white horse upon the mountains, that was another woman. That was Kurt's wife.

She shook her head. "I can't marry you, Kurt," she said.

His finger, moving along the Himalayas, stopped. "No? Still no, Eleanor?"

She nodded.

"Why not, Eleanor?" he asked gently.

"I—cannot," she said. "I don't want to, Kurt."

He folded the maps slowly and put them in his pocket again.

"You don't want to marry *me*, perhaps," he suggested.

"I don't want to marry anybody," she said.

He thought a moment. "That," he said, "requires explanation to me, Eleanor. Not to want to marry *me* I can understand. I am so big, I am—well, yes, I am an American now with all these papers, but still I am very new. I have no graces, I blunder into your nice rooms like the rhinoceros. But not to want to marry anybody—no, it is not natural."

"Perhaps I am not quite a natural woman," she said. Her lips trembled a little when she made them smile.

"You? With those lips and eyes?" Kurt exclaimed. "Never will I believe that! When I first met you at that silly dinner table—such a fool he was, I can't remember his name—"

"Jeremy Prescott, the great critic and—" she murmured.

"Great conceited fool," he went on, "and no one was real except you. You sat there so quiet, like an intelligent mouse."

"I'm not a mouse!" she exclaimed in indignation.

"No, and I know that now," he said. "You are a stubborn woman and I love you. . . . Come! Let us go to your place and talk. You will talk and I will find out why you don't want to marry. For I see the trouble now. If you don't want to marry at all, how can you want to marry *me*? I see that. . . . Waiter!"

He paid the bill in great haste and hurried her into her coat.

"We shall walk," he exclaimed. "I feel faster on my own feet. Besides, the good air will clear our heads for better understanding."

He put his hand in her arm and swung his stride to hers. It was a glorious day. The streets were full of cheerful glowing people. The winter was over and spring was ahead and summer to come. The tall buildings were towers of alabaster against a sapphire sky. She was suddenly very contented.

"There is nothing to talk about," she said, turning her face upward toward his. "I am quite happy here. If I am happy in New York, why should I go to the Himalayas?"

"With me," said Kurt gently.

"If I am happy alone—"

"You are not happier without me," said Kurt, and hurried her along.

In her bedroom alone she took off her hat before the mirror and washed her hands and smoothed her hair. Then she went to the window and stood looking down into the street. Kurt was waiting for her in the living room, Kurt with his Himalayas and his romance and the hugeness of mountains in him, mountains and miles of sunshine and air. He was always clamoring for air. She smiled, thinking of it. He never went into a room without throwing up a window to sit by. There was no one like him. He deserved everything of her—everything she could give him. If she could not give him love, she could give him at least the truth. She made up her mind swiftly. She would tell him everything, the whole and simple truth of why she would not marry anybody. She would tell him her whole life. He deserved to understand her fully. And then their friendship could go on, precious upon sure foundations. She turned swiftly toward the door.

But it was very hard to begin. She had never told Kurt much about that other first self of hers. Why should she until now talk about a woman who was dead? She sat down in the blue chair. The thin blue curtains were waving in the wind from the open window and by it Kurt was sitting waiting for her, his thick hair ruffling. She sat looking at him.

"Well?" he said, and smiled at her warmly.

"How shall I begin?" she said.

"As you will," he replied. "I am good at collecting bits of data and piecing them into a whole. It is my business as a scientist!"

She waited and stared down at her clasped ringless hands.

"Perhaps I had better begin like this," she said slowly. "My husband said to me, 'You must choose between your writing or me.' " She glanced at him.

He sat quite still, the wind ruffling his hair, his face vivid with confidence, waiting. She looked down at her hands again.

"It didn't come to that choice at once," she went on. She would not look at him again. She would just go straight ahead. "He said that to me one night. We quarreled unexpectedly after dinner. I see now there had been many small things before which I had scarcely noticed until that night. But they had mounted, unseen." She paused. "What you must understand, Kurt, is that I was quite another woman then. I was in love with my husband. I was happily married. I never dreamed that anything could disturb my marriage. Hartley loved me. I never doubted it. I can't tell you now exactly how it all came about. If I could have given up my writing it would have been simple enough. But I found I couldn't."

She reflected a moment. "I had a friend—Myra said she couldn't imagine why not. I couldn't tell her. But I know that if I had given it up I would slowly have died. I'd have gone on being Hartley's wife, and dying. I don't know why. I don't care for personal success or money or fame. I don't think the world is any better off because of my books. I have to go on for myself. It's necessity for life and growth—the exercise of a function for which I was made."

"I can understand that, my Eleanor," said Kurt gently. He who usually was so restless, so full of vigorous movement, now was still. He was one who could not be ignored in a room, because he was so big, his voice so strong, his eyes so electric. Yet now he had withdrawn himself so that he was no intrusion upon her story. She could go back to those years undisturbed by his presence today.

"He gave me that dreadful choice one night, but I would not choose. I didn't believe I *had* to choose. I thought, 'I will let this moment pass and show him how much I love him. I won't let him see me working. I'll try to arrange all of this part of my life at hours when he is away.'

"But it was not quite possible. The second book was successful, too. I couldn't help being glad, though by then I was so frightened that I said nothing at all to him about it. But other people did. They congratulated him, they said silly things like, 'How does it feel to be the husband of a famous woman, Hartley?' and they'd say, 'I should think you'd stop slaving for a salary when your wife can pay the bills.' "

She paused, frowning. "Money—that was another thing. He was so—confusing about it. He didn't like my earning so much more than he did. He wanted me to put everything into a joint account, because, he said, if I died and had a personal account it would make everything hard for him. I didn't care about money—I did as he said. But then he seemed to feel once it was in the bank it all belonged to him. Once I wanted to give something—quite a lot—to the orphanage. We'd never had children and he didn't want to adopt one—

he said it couldn't be the same as his own. So I used to go over to the orphanage sometimes to play with the children. They needed a new wing for the babies and I wanted to give it to them. But he didn't."

"Ha!" said Kurt shortly and stirred in his chair.

"It wasn't that he really minded the orphanage having the money," she said quickly. "He wasn't mean. It was—this all came to me afterward—that he didn't want me to think I could give away a lot of money—by myself."

"Your money!" Kurt said.

"No, that was it—*not* mine," she answered. "Because he thought of me as his and so what was mine was his, too. He kept saying, 'We're one person. You mustn't do things by yourself.' But it didn't occur to me to say until long after, 'You do things by yourself.' Buying stocks, for instance—he didn't tell me."

"Beast!" said Kurt.

But she shook her head. "No, I'm not telling it rightly if you say that. He wasn't a beast. He was good. People looked up to him, and so did I. He could be very charming, too— in his way. I was very happy—you must realize that, Kurt. I didn't feel at all misunderstood or anything like that. No, I think it was that he had always thought of me as belonging to him, my every thought his, you know—and then he began to feel I wasn't altogether his. At first I am sure it was just a hurt, a feeling of separation. He didn't have it as long as I was just writing little things and reading them to him. It was after *Storm Tonight.* Then everybody was writing and talking and people kept coming. It was as though the world had smashed down our front door and swarmed into our quiet house. . . . And I couldn't help it. The thing was done. I hadn't dreamed of it. I wrote as inevitably as I breathed and sent it away to be a book, hoping, naturally, it was good enough. The book, printed and bound, in my hand, was the end to me, as the clay figure cast into bronze is to the sculptor. I never thought of or wanted more. The door was smashed down before I knew it, and no one could put it up again."

Kurt stirred impatiently. "If you could have, my Eleanor, it would have done no good. The gift—it was there. You would never have been yourself, your whole self, with your gift locked and idle."

She looked at him, surprised. "You see that, Kurt?"

He laughed, a loud short laugh. "I see you have the right to be yourself!" he retorted.

"Yes," she said, pondering. "It took me a long time to see it, and a still longer time to see that if I were not myself not even Hartley would be happy with me. But still I would not choose."

She waited a little while, remembering. "I loved our life very much. I loved the house—every room, every bit of furniture, the view from every window. That woman who was Hartley's wife will always haunt that house. She couldn't have lived here like this, alone, twenty stories high, in New York. Why, she would have been afraid even to spend the night alone! But out of her another woman was born, shrinkingly, unwillingly. But Hartley drove her to birth, not knowing what he did."

"I say 'Beast!' " Kurt whispered strongly.

"No, Kurt!" she cried impatiently. "You can't understand me if you don't understand him. You must understand! You might have been the same yourself!"

"I?" he exclaimed incredulously. "I, who love you?"

"Hartley loved me, too," she said.

"He loved his wife—not you," he retorted.

She pondered this. "Perhaps you are right," she said. "Perhaps he only loved me because I was his wife. But I felt oppressed with guilt for the change in him. I thought, 'If I had been as he thought I was, he would have gone on growing like a straight tree. But I've warped him. I've pulled him crooked.' For he began to grow strange, Kurt. And I bore it because I thought it was my fault."

She stopped to wet her dry lips.

"And then?" said Kurt. His big thin hands were clenched on his crossed knees.

"I kept not choosing, you see. That was when I was writing *The Waking Wind.* I couldn't stop. And I couldn't give him up. I didn't think seriously I'd have to choose. Sometimes I thought I could just write a few more things I had in my head and then give it up. And all the time he grew harder, different. Everything was wrong—every small thing, I mean. I couldn't say anything, especially before other people, without his correcting me. I couldn't put a flower in a vase without his suggesting something. I gave up driving the car. He hated my clothes and he said he wanted my hair done differently. But I couldn't find any new way to suit him. I could scarcely breathe. I felt in prison. The only moment I was free was when he was gone and I was in my room working. We never mentioned it."

Kurt was sitting upright staring at her, breathing hard, his lips clamped shut.

But she went on.

"The horrible thing is that I knew I'd done it to him. And I couldn't stop. When I was working I was free—only when I was working."

She was trembling all over, but she went on, hurrying.

"When *The Waking Wind* came out, it was more successful than the first book. It was impossible to hide it from him. And as he knew—and I knew—I saw the choice was made. I hadn't made it, nor had he. But the woman I now am had been born, had grown, and was more than that other woman. And he knew it. I didn't need to say a word. We sat together one evening as we had so often sat, and I knew that Hartley's wife was dead. If he could love me, the woman I am, I could live with him in love. Because, I thought, if he could love *me*, then he was the man for me. He would have grown, too. So I said that to him.

"I said, 'Hartley, do you love me at all?'

"And he said, 'You don't seem the same person any more.'

"I was still new enough to be terribly frightened by the way he looked and spoke—so cold, so cold! And I said, 'I love *you*, Hartley.' And he said, 'Ah, but *I* haven't changed.' What could I say, then, but what I said? I said, 'There can't be room for me here in your home, then, Hartley. I had better go away.' He didn't say a word. He put his head in his hands. I stood up. I couldn't believe he wouldn't speak—wouldn't cry out, 'Oh, my darling, stay, stay!' I put my hand on his shoulder. But he didn't speak or move. So I went upstairs and put some things together and came downstairs. He was still sitting there. And I went out and got into the car. The little dog jumped up and wanted to come, too. But I didn't want even the little dog. I had to be alone, alone. I came away and I never went back."

She swallowed hard. "I never saw him again, except once, the day of his mother's funeral. When he married last year, I cried a little—but I was glad."

She was shivering and suddenly cold, as though she had taken off garments. She did not look up. She must wait until she stopped shivering. But Kurt had leaped out of his chair. His arms were about her, warm and close. He lifted her to her feet against him. His voice was hurrying.

"And so, now will you let me ask you to marry me? It is you I want to marry—this woman, you. I could never have loved that wife of Hartley. I love you as now you are, the true you!"

It was so blessed to be warm, to be supported, to be held hard against a strong body, that she was dazed with it. She had never let him hold her before. She was afraid of his nearness, afraid of the step beyond. They were not children experimenting with kiss and caress. These things had too profound a potency for common use. Now she stood accepting for a moment this shelter of his arms about her, her cheek upon his breast.

"Oh, Kurt!" she whispered. She closed her eyes—and immediately was afraid. What was she doing here in Kurt's arms?

She might in a moment like this lose what she valued most, that freedom to be herself which had cost her so much. For if she married Kurt she would then become Kurt's wife. And how was Kurt's wife better than Hartley's? She drew herself fiercely out of his arms.

"You wouldn't like me if I married you, though, Kurt. If I were your wife you'd want me to see to the meals and keep the house running and have things as you like them. And I'd want to do all those things, dear Kurt! But inside of me, this me I am would be straining and straining against your wife. No, no! I shan't marry. A woman like me, such a craving to create, must not marry. I learned that once for all."

She was quite away from him now. He was standing there as though she had stabbed him, staring at her, his face white.

"So! You think I am only another man—another Hartley man!" He was breathing hard. She put out her hand quickly, but he did not take it. He rushed on. "You don't believe me when I say—" He seized her by the shoulder and shook her a little. "Do you think I care about food—I who eat what there is for months on end—or I do not eat? Do you think I care about houses and—and such stuff? Listen to me while I tell you again I love you! I want you to marry me, I want to marry you. You will do your work, I will do my work, and we will leave each other alone because we love each other—" His voice softened. He took her hand and pulled her to the sofa beside him. "My Eleanor, there is a love which is satisfied only when the beloved is most free and most happy and most herself. I don't want to shape you and change you. I cannot be jealous of you, I can only respect you and be proud of you. I don't ask you to be my wife. I ask you to marry me. I don't want a wife—I want *you!*"

She listened, drinking in his words, wondering, doubting.

"It's beautiful—what you say," she said, "but I don't quite believe it. I wish I could—as I wish I could believe in heaven. But I know that when we began living together, inevitably

I'd take the woman's place. And the woman's place is to adjust, to adapt, to meet demands—"

"I demand nothing," Kurt said quickly.

"Dear Kurt, you wouldn't know you were demanding."

By every word she said she was strengthening herself and confirming herself. She was beginning to feel safe again, caught back from that moment in Kurt's arms. She had been nearly lost. Strange how nearly instinctive it was to want shelter! But shelter was partly prison, too. She drew a long breath and smiled at him.

But before he could speak Mattie knocked upon the door. She knew Mattie's bony knock, and she was glad of it for once.

"Come in, Mattie!" she called.

Mattie's head was thrust in. "Miss Eleanor, Miss Myra done telephone while you was gone she's comin' up to see you this aft'noon. I reckon she be hyeah purty soon. Want I should make tea?"

"Myra? . . . Yes, that would be nice."

"Yas'm."

Mattie shut the door, and Eleanor turned to Kurt. "Stay, Kurt, too. You'll like Myra." And Myra would be a help to her against him, she thought.

"No," he said, "no, I won't stay." He rose at that very moment. "No, I must go and think by myself again."

She rose, sorry for him. "Think what? There isn't anything to think about any more."

"There is everything," he said. "I see now what I have to think. I must think how to show you what I mean when I say marriage—our marriage."

"Kurt, please!" she begged him.

"No, don't be troubled, Eleanor. It is my problem, not yours. I see how you feel. I don't blame you. But you must see more, and I must show you. So! I will not ask you to marry me again until you see what I mean. Then I will ask you one more time. If then you say no, my Eleanor, it is to say it is I you cannot love."

The doorbell rang. There was a bustle in the hall. A gay voice cried, "Mattie, you good-for-nothing, you haven't gone and made cheese biscuits! I smell them!"

"So I do not say goodbye, Eleanor."

"No, Kurt."

"So!"

He took her hand in both of his, and she suddenly bent her head and laid her cheek upon them. "If I could have married anyone, I could have thought of no one else than you, Kurt, but—"

"Yes—no more—I see it!"

He smiled in his old undismayed fashion and whispered gaily, "Now I will tiptoe this way while she comes that way!" He disappeared into the little dining room.

She was glad the door opened immediately. She was glad to see Myra, full-blown and rosy and beaming with pleasure.

"Well, my dear!" Myra kissed both her cheeks. "I just don't care if you are famous and busy and everything else, I just have to see you once in a while! And Mattie says she's made cheese biscuits for me! I called up ahead *hoping* that if she knew I was coming—"

"I was just wishing someone would come," said Eleanor, smiling. "I'm going to be alone all evening."

"Oh, my dear! I couldn't possibly just go away like that— Hal would think I'd left him if he didn't find me when he came in. I've been shopping all day—" She was flinging off her coat, her hat, and her gloves were on the floor. Eleanor stooped to pick them up. "Oh, dear," Myra cried, "I'm always dropping— Oh, it's so good to see you, Nora darling. I miss you so! I never pass your house without feeling it unbelievable that you aren't there!"

She sat down and fluffed her short dark hair with her fingers. She laughed suddenly. "I must tell you something, Eleanor.

I couldn't tell every woman. But you have a sense of humor. Elsa—you know—she's so much like you it's funny—like what you were, rather. She's not a bit like you are now. I never saw anybody change so much. But, my dear, the way she talks, the way she moves—especially the way she looks at Hartley—is so much like you used to do. And nothing is changed—in the house, I mean."

"Why should it be?" said Eleanor. "It was always as Hartley wanted it. I suppose it still is."

"You aren't bitter, are you?" Myra asked, her black eyes widening.

"Not in the least," said Eleanor, composed. She began pouring the tea. "You like cream, don't you, Myra? And there are the cheese biscuits! Mattie always has them buttered. No, how can I be bitter, Myra, when I made my own choice?"

She thought to herself, "I made that choice again today."

"Yes, of course," said Myra. "But isn't it funny about Elsa?"

Eleanor smiled without reply. One didn't need to reply to Myra. She went on and on.

"I must say, Eleanor, I don't know whether I envy you or pity you—it depends on my mood, I think. When Hal comes in cross and wants this and that, and the children are nasty, I must say I think of you able to do exactly as you please—and other times when things are right again, I think how awful it would be to leave home and live without my husband and children—so lonely! Of course you didn't have children, which is a mercy—though if you had—"

Eleanor half listened, smiling, pouring tea, passing the biscuits. The afternoon wore on. The sky grew soft with sunset.

"There—I've got to go." Myra was putting on her hat. "It's been lovely to come into this quiet room and just talk."

"I'm glad you came this particular day," said Eleanor.

But when Myra was ready to go she leaned over impulsively and took Eleanor's face between her two hands and gazed into her eyes. "Sure you're happy?" she asked.

"Sure," said Eleanor steadily.

Myra examined her.

"It's queer—but I believe you are," she said and dropped her hands. "Well, goodbye, you dear thing!"

"Goodbye," said Eleanor.

So the room was empty again, and she was glad to have it so. Myra had driven out Kurt, and now Myra too was gone. She was alone. But only for a moment—there came welling up in her the old beloved desire. She said to Mattie, who had come in to clear away the tea, "Mattie, I'm going to work all evening. Bring my dinner in on a tray and set it beside me and go away without saying a word."

"Yas'm, Miss Eleanor," said Mattie with deference.

She sat down and the day was swept away, and with it herself. Her own people came crowding into the room. She began to write quickly, eagerly, and Kurt was as though he had never been. The sun set and night fell, but she did not know it and did not care. Under her fingers life was shaping itself. She was making life.

Waking the next day at noon, she heard Mattie tiptoeing about the door.

"Come in, Mattie!" she called sleepily. There was agitation in Mattie's step.

The door opened and Mattie's head came in. "I didn't want to wake you," Mattie began.

"Come in, Mattie—don't be a Cheshire cat," Eleanor said gaily. It was glorious to wake up after a bout of work, to wake with that feeling of accomplishment and completeness.

"A telegram done come and I didn't give it to you since you get 'em every day, and then another and another, till there is four and I'm desprit—'cause they's all from the same place. The telefoam keeps a-ringin' and every time it's the same man."

"Not Mr. Stenson?" Eleanor asked.

"No'm, it's Mr. Brady."

"Let me see the telegrams," said Eleanor. She yawned and

sat up. Mr. Brady was her agent. She tore open the yellow envelope.

"Fas' as the telefoam ring, the boy'd bring one of 'em," Mattie said.

"It's only business," said Eleanor, reading.

"Of all the nuisances!" said Mattie, disappointed. "Well, I'll go and git your breakfast, then." She tiptoed heavily away.

Eleanor spread the telegrams out before her. They all said the same thing. They all gave her the chance she had never even dreamed of. Michael Bredon, the great producer, wanted her to dramatize *Storm Tonight*. She could not believe it. But there it was. "Bredon believes book will be great play. Wants immediate reply."

How lucky, how lucky that yesterday in Kurt's arms she had not yielded! She had been trembling on the edge of love. Even at this moment something in her was ready to fall in love with Kurt. She might have been lost again in love. But now this would save her. She could not possibly go to the Himalayas on a honeymoon when there was a play to be written and produced. It would be months before she could think of anything else. "October production urgent," one of the telegrams said. She took up the telephone receiver beside her bed, dialed, and began to dictate quickly. "Western Union? Yes—Brady—yes—that's the address. Tell Bredon I accept with delight and gratitude. Eleanor Dane."

It was as well, she thought, as day passed after day, that Kurt saw her now as she was, in the fever and joy of her work. She made no pretense of leisure. She was desperately busy, wildly absorbed. He came, never to stay long, but he came often. Sometimes she looked up from her desk out of a maze of her people and their talk to see Kurt standing at the door, smiling, gazing at her. Sometimes she could not speak, she was so far away. She looked and turned back to the clamoring of her own voices and whether he stayed or went she did not know. Once, struggling toward him, she cried, "Kurt!" But he put his finger to his lips and when she looked up again he was gone.

Thus it went while she took her people out of the book and made them act out their life upon a stage. It was new technique and she loved it for its nearness to life. She could throw away the pages of her own telling of woods and skies and homes and the pages of how this one was and how that one lived and moved. Instead she saw movement, heard voices, in time and space. She studied light and darkness, measured the reality of lightnings, weighed the sounds of winds, and criticized thunders. She laughed aloud to herself at night in the few hours she had for sleep. "I'm play-acting myself," she said to herself, "play-acting I'm God." She had never been so happy, sleeping in fragments, eating when she could, and hour after hour making and shaping, writing and rewriting. In the casting office, she gazed at hundreds of actors, men and women, young and old, to find at last among them the faces, the minds, the shapes, for her voices. Whether she was alive or not she did not think. She gave herself up as she had never given herself even to be Hartley's wife. If she thought of Kurt it was as of someone she had known long ago, grateful only that she had told him who she was and finished with him before this came.

Summer came and went and September began, feverish with rehearsals. Bredon was ferocious, comprehending, exacting. He was a whip to compel perfection. Under his development of her play she continually saw new nuances, new sharpening. She was always at rehearsal, watching out of the darkness of the empty theater, watching to see what she had done.

Out of the chaos of the beginning she watched shape and form grow until all was order—and what did not fit the order was discarded. She learned, in a discipline more severe than any she had ever known, to see a whole scene she loved thrown aside because it did not sweep the story onward. The faults in her work stared at her, acted upon a stage, and she was the first to cry out from the darkness where she sat alone, "Take that out—all of it—it's not right!"

Bredon would turn a sour profile to growl at her, "You'll make a play yet!"

She smiled, undisturbed. "I *have* a play!" she cried to him across the spaces.

"Maybe—maybe!" He granted her a little more each day. "Yes, it's better—we'll have something at the end, but a lot of work yet. . . ."

And so until at last he said, "Now we have it. Your part is done." Then, for the first time in months, she knew where she was and how she was.

She was still alive, a human creature. She was tired, she was happy. She needed to sleep and sleep. She stumbled into her door one night and Mattie came running.

"Miss Eleanor, you's sick!"

"No! I'm wonderful—happy as anything—only starved, sleepy. I want a bath and a lot of food and sleep. Let me sleep until I wake."

"Thank goo'ness!" Mattie cried. "Well, thank goo'ness, Miss Eleanor!"

She seized Eleanor's hand and led her into her room and helped her undress and set the tub running.

"Now, then—I throwed in a double han'ful of the verbena salts. You soak yourself good."

Half asleep, Eleanor lay in softened fragrant water. Now at last her people let her be. They had all gone trooping out of her mind, laughing, singing, weeping, into their own life. They could live without her now. Their life would go on, strong and sufficient for reality.

"It's a good play," she murmured. "I did a good piece of work. I did what I wanted to do."

Clean, fed, in her own bed, she lay down to sleep until she waked. Mattie drew down the shades.

"Mattie," she muttered from the bed, "what time is it? I haven't known for a long time."

"It's eight o'clock in de mawnin', honey," Mattie said.

"Eight o'clock in the morning! Why, it's the time I get up usually!"

"You just shut yo eyes," said Mattie severely. "You just et a chicken dinner I made for you yistiddy and you didn't show up. Far as you's concerned, honey, it's daid of night!"

It took a long time to wake up. She had a memory of eating sometime or other again—perhaps more than once—of Mattie at her with hot cocoa and an egg—but she did not wake up. She slept as dreamlessly as death. When she woke she woke fully and clearly, her body light with rest, relaxed with the freedom of her spirit's content. The shades were bright with the sunshine of late afternoon. What day it was she did not know. She looked at her little clock—half past four.

She got up and drew up the shades. Outside, everything was going on as usual. Cars were streaming back and forth, people walking in the gay light, life going on while she had been sleeping. It was good to come back to it, rested and ready. She was eager to join into it again. The papers—she wanted to read newspapers and know what was happening—what was everybody doing?

She rang the bell and when Mattie ran to her door she laughed.

"I'm awake at last, Mattie! Bring me my letters and all the papers! And tell me who has been here to see me! I feel as if I'd been in another country!"

Mattie, bringing back the letters and a pile of unopened papers, said, "Ain't hardly been anybody here, Miss Eleanor."

Eleanor, tearing open wrappers, glancing at letters, smiled. "One of these days I'm going to have to stop long enough to make myself some friends for my old age."

"Indeed and you should, Miss Eleanor. Other girls hyeah in this house says, 'Who you wukkin' for?' I says, proud as can be, 'I wuks for Miss Eleanor Dane,' and they says, 'My, you mus' have a gay life!' and I says, 'Who—me? It's like—' "

"Yes, Mattie, I know. Someday—"

"Ain't nobody come except Mr. Stenson, and even he doan come in any more. He come to de do' and says, 'Is she all right?' and I says—"

"Ah, Kurt—perhaps there's a letter from him!"

She searched through the envelopes. No, there was nothing.

"I must call him up," she said. "After breakfast—if this can be breakfast, Mattie."

"Far as you's concerned," Mattie mumbled, hastening away.

So she went on reading while she waited for her tray, while she ate. There was nothing in the letters—the bills, the few fan letters, the many begging letters—nothing from anyone she knew. Yes, she really must stop and make some friends. She picked up an English weekly Kurt sent her regularly. She had not looked at it for a long time, but Kurt said it was the only place to find news not American. She missed Kurt a little, now that she had time to stop and think about anybody. Kurt was the only friend she had. She'd telephone— and at that instant her eyes fell on a paragraph. "Hardinger Expedition Sets Off." That was Kurt's expedition! Why, Kurt had left the country without a word! And why, she demanded of herself, would Kurt feel he had to tell her? Probably he had tried to tell her and she— She read on quickly. "The expedition leaves London today, headed by Franz Sobel. It was hoped until the last moment that Kurt Stenson, the well-known naturalist, would take command, but Mr. Stenson cabled his regrets from New York."

"Oh, Kurt!" she exclaimed aloud. "Of all foolishness!" He had not gone! She'd been hurt a moment ago when she'd thought he had gone and now she was angry because he had not—a nice consistent sort of woman she was! She reached for the telephone, dialed, waited. The bell in Kurt's little tall house, wedged between two taller buildings, rang perseveringly. She waited. He lived there quite alone except for Lars, the old Swede who did for him. But there was not even any Lars. She hung up at last. "They're both out," she thought.

She finished her tray and telephoned again. But no one answered.

She hung up then, at a loss. Lars, at least, should be at home, cooking Kurt's dinner. Lars was always at home, hating New York. Once when she had gone to Kurt's for tea, Kurt had said, "Lars, he doesn't even like to go out and buy my little beefsteak. He bribes the cook next door for anything he can't telephone."

Lars smiled and nodded. "I stay home—I don't get lost," he said. "I go out, I don't come back so good."

She was suddenly restless, thinking of them. "I'll get up," she resolved. "I'll walk over there myself and find out."

She sprang out of bed, bathed, and put on her green suit that Kurt liked, and pulled on the small tight brown hat. She looked well again, rested and ready. But it was the rest that came only when she was content with her work done, a deep rest that was more than body. It had been worth it. Next week the play opened, but she was not afraid. Her best was good enough so she need not be afraid.

She walked quickly and lightly down the street. The first chill of coming autumn was in the brilliant dying sunshine. The summer had gone in such a daze that she could not remember it. She did not know whether she had been hot or not. Had Kurt been here in the city all summer? He hated summer, especially city summer. He was a man of the north, loving snow and cold. Ah, she should have stopped a moment to see that he was going away! She would have made him go on his beloved expedition. Why, he had been talking about the little flowers in the Himalayas ever since she had known him! Even that first night, she remembered, at the stupid dinner, he had said, "But the dream of my life is to find a certain little blue flower. It grows in the snow, in the Himalayas—seldom seen, never studied. I shall go there one day."

She stopped in front of his house. It looked quite closed. She went up the steps and rang the bell. But the door did not open. She rang again and again. But no one came.

There was nothing to do, then, but walk home again. She walked a few blocks and then found herself tired. Some vigor had gone out of the air. Perhaps it was the twilight. She was one of those who always found twilight saddening. Kurt, discovering this restlessness in her at the coming of night, used often to come and see her then, and with him she did not notice the edging darkness. But now he was gone, and without a word.

She motioned to a taxi and climbed in and sat, very aloof, while the car darted down the street. She might as well face it. She was lonely. Now that she did not know where Kurt was, she missed him. She even longed for him a little, as one might for a friend expected and gone. If she could have known he was away on the expedition, she would not have minded. She would have known he was there, in the world, enjoying his work, his life, and they would meet again. But now—no one knew—she did not know where to turn. Even though she did not want to marry him, Kurt could not just drop out of her life like this.

But going up in the familiar elevator she thought, "Of course he will come back. Kurt couldn't be alive and not come back to tell me so." She smiled to herself, feeling comfort creeping back. Kurt would propose to her doubtless again and again. It would be almost worth the trouble of his proposals to have him back and know he was all right. When he was there she could forget him, but when he was gone she was miserable. She thought this over rather gravely as she stood waiting for Mattie to open the door. What did it mean?

There was no time to answer herself. The door opened at once. Mattie stood there, her eyes rolling.

"Miss Eleanor, they's a lady here. I don' know ef you want to see her. I says—"

"Who is she?"

"Honey, I hate to tell you. I cain't think what for she—"

"What's her name?"

"Miss Eleanor, it's Mrs.—I declare, I cain't say it—it's *your* name, honey! She says she's Mrs. Bainbridge!"

Eleanor went toward the living-room door and looked in. A young fair-haired woman was sitting in the blue chair. She was reading a magazine, but now she looked up.

"Good evening," she said in a soft and hesitating voice.

"Elsa Freed!" said Eleanor.

III

She had known Elsa Freed so little that when Myra said, "Eleanor, Hartley's going to marry that little Elsa Freed," she said, "Elsa Freed? Have I ever met her?" Of course, she told her startled heart, of course he would marry again.

And Myra said, "Don't you remember that blonde little girl Hartley danced with one New Year's Eve at our house? It was—let me see—the year I had my silver sequin evening gown."

"Yes, I remember," Eleanor said.

Of course she wanted Hartley to be happy. She remembered the dance. That night, going to bed, she had said to him, "That was such a pretty girl, Hartley, the one with the fair hair."

Hartley said, "Her father is the director who was chosen in old Mr. Blackman's place." Mr. Blackman was dead.

"Didn't you think her pretty, Hartley?" she asked.

"I didn't look at her—Myra told me to ask her," Hartley said, yawning.

"Ah, she was very pretty!" Eleanor cried. "I love pretty people!"

She sat smiling, remembering the fresh young face, the clear skin, the bright blue eyes. She'd keep the memory of that young creature and put it in a story one day, and clothe with that beauty another soul. So when Myra said, "Elsa Freed," she remembered.

"I hope she's not too young for Hartley," she said anxiously to Myra.

Myra laughed loudly. "Eleanor, if you aren't the funniest woman! What does it matter to you?"

"I don't hate Hartley, Myra," she answered, surprised.

"Oh, dear," cried Myra, wiping her eyes. "Well, you needn't worry about Hartley, I should say."

That was all she had ever heard. At first, when the marriage was announced, she could not keep from thinking of another woman in her room, using her things, moving about the house which had once been hers. But after a while that went away, too.

And now, here this woman was, sitting in Eleanor's own living room.

She looked up from a magazine. "Good evening," she said in a soft fresh voice.

"Elsa Freed!" Eleanor exclaimed.

They stared at each other.

"I've wondered how you looked now," Elsa Freed said. "Hartley never says a word about you."

Eleanor sat down and lit a cigarette. "Why should he?" she replied calmly. "I've gone away."

Elsa shook her short fair hair childishly. "I keep wondering if you have," she said. "I mean—he can't have forgotten all those years."

"Yes, he can," Eleanor said. "You don't know him yet if you think he isn't able to forget what he doesn't want to remember. You may be quite sure that nothing of me is left in him. He's your husband—a very devoted one, I know."

She smoked the cigarette slowly. She was afraid at first that she would not be able to be calm. But she was able. She could be quite aloof from these two, Elsa Freed and her husband.

"Oh, he's devoted enough," Elsa said. She moved restlessly and put the magazine on the table. "You're probably wondering why on earth I am here," she said suddenly. "It is queer—my coming."

"Nothing is queer," said Eleanor. "I don't know why you have come, but if there is anything I can do for you, I will do it."

"Do you mind if I take off my hat?" Elsa asked.

"Not in the least."

The girl took off her small blue hat. She was all in blue, the soft pastel blue that was Hartley's favorite color. She ran her fingers through her hair and lit a cigarette.

"There!" she said. "Now—I'll tell you why I've come, Miss Dane. That's what you like to be called, isn't it? I know because I read everything I can find about you."

"That was my own name—before I was married," Eleanor said gently. She felt old enough to be the mother of Hartley's wife.

"I know—it's a lovely name. I've admired you so. I think your books are wonderful! I like the first one best, only I wish you hadn't let the girl die. I cried like anything and Hartley asked me why my eyes were so red, and I said I thought I was getting a cold. I couldn't tell him. I keep your books hidden. It's queer, but we never talk about you. But I think about you such a lot. Sometimes when Hartley's making love to me, even, I think, 'I wonder if it was like this with her.'"

"Don't!" Eleanor cried in a low voice.

"Oh, I don't mind!" Elsa Freed's eyes opened very wide. "Hartley makes love beautifully. No, I mean, I just want you to know I do admire you tremendously. I could no more be jealous of you than I could of—oh, the Queen of England! One of my friends said to me, 'I should think you'd be jealous of her.' But I'm not. I know Hartley loves me. And I have my own points, haven't I?" She looked at Eleanor and smiled, a wide frank smile.

"Indeed, yes," said Eleanor. It was impossible to dislike this girl. She was so very pretty and still so young. She would always be young. Hartley could—

"No," the girl began again eagerly, "what I said to myself was, 'She'—that's you—'she's the very person to help me. She knows exactly what I'm up against. And anybody who can work things between people the way she does in her books will know how to help me work it out with Hartley.' "

Eleanor drew a breath. What was this girl saying? What preposterous task was this set before her, to reconcile some difference between Hartley and his wife? She wet her lips and said very quietly, "I'm really not a very good person to help you, I'm afraid. I couldn't help myself. I mean—I didn't know what to do."

"But you had something else to do," the girl said eagerly. "I can't do anything. I can't write or sing or do anything to make a career. You have such a wonderful life of your own. People want to know you and you must have so much fun. But I haven't anything. I'm just me."

Eleanor was suddenly very sorry for Hartley. Poor Hartley—if the same thing should happen to him again, it would be more somehow than she could bear. If she could save his wife for him, perhaps it would make up to him for herself.

"Perhaps I *can* help you," she said gently. "Suppose you tell me just what is wrong."

Elsa lit another cigarette. She seemed so casual, but she was trembling. Eleanor saw her slender hands tremble and under the close blue skirt her knees were trembling. But she smoked with young bravado.

"Probably he wasn't the same way with you," she said. "I can't imagine his being the same. I mean, you look as though no one could—could tell you what to do all the time."

"Does Hartley do that?" She found she could not possibly tell this girl anything about the woman who had been Hartley's wife. She could not have any part now in Hartley. It was revolting to think that she was a third, however shadowy, in their marriage. Eleanor Dane—she was simply Eleanor Dane, a casual acquaintance to whom a girl had turned for advice. Many girls wrote letters to her saying, "I've read all your books and I believe you can tell me what to do. I am in love, but—" This was just one of those girls.

"He's always telling me what to do." Elsa's eyes were full of rushing tears, but she kept her voice steady. "At first I thought it was because—well, he was quite a lot in love with me."

"Aren't you in love with him?"

"Yes—of course I am. Sometimes I'm terribly in love with him. But sometimes I just feel smothered."

"When did you begin to feel so?" She was making her voice as cold as a physician's. It helped Elsa. She winked back the tears.

"At first I didn't mind. It was rather fun having somebody so—so absorbed in me. I mean, it was fun to know he'd notice every least thing I did—it was exciting. I was awfully in love, too. He's good-looking, don't you think, Miss Dane?"

"Yes, he is," said Eleanor.

"But after a while—it made me feel as though I wasn't myself. I was Mrs. Hartley Bainbridge and not Elsa Freed any more. Then I thought, 'Well, I suppose that's marriage.' And I talked a little—not much—to some of my married friends and they all said the same thing. One of them said, 'It's a job. I have to be on duty all the time Tom's home. That's what I get paid for.' Well, that was sense, I thought. Everybody has some sort of job. So I said, 'My job is to be Hartley's wife.' "

She looked at Eleanor.

"Yes?" said Eleanor.

"But I guess I'm sick of my job, Miss Dane. I don't know what's the matter with me. But take tonight—Hartley had a business dinner tonight and we had to come to New York. I'm supposed to be at a theater with a girl I knew in college. But I'd put out a tan dress to wear and Hartley saw it and said, 'Wear the blue one, Elsa. It's much more becoming.' And I wanted to say, 'Hartley, I've decided on the tan,' but I couldn't. I just went on meekly and put on this thing. And I want to let my hair grow and roll it at the back, but he likes it this way. And if he wants me to go to a dinner or something, I have to go. And he always introduces me, 'This is my wife,' until I feel I'm just nothing."

The tears were in her eyes again and she was rushing on. "Everything is the same. I've got to be what he wants all the time, go where he says to go, be the sort of person he wants his wife to be. Miss Dane, I envy you so! If I could just earn my living and have my own apartment and be myself!"

Hartley's wife—Hartley's wife! And what could she say?

"These are all small things," she said gently. "Go on—tell me how he is to you. Is he generous with you? Does he give you money and pretty clothes? That's a lovely suit you are wearing—it *is* becoming to you. Your eyes look like—there is a beautiful little blue flower that grows in the snow in the Himalayas and your eyes look like that."

Elsa smiled. "Do they really? Hartley bought this for me because of my eyes. Yes, he gives me plenty of money. But money's not everything."

"No," Eleanor agreed. She was silent a moment. "Do you like the house? I used to think it the loveliest place, especially at night, in the living room, with those heavy gold curtains drawn and the great fireplace going."

"Oh, I do love the house!" Elsa cried. "And don't you love the garden? That clump of lilies-of-the-valley under the old yews."

"And the wisteria," said Eleanor.

"Yes, and the little marble pool."

"Hartley's grandfather built that," said Eleanor, "and he brought that winged Cupid from Italy. I always thought the white shadow in the water so lovely. I miss not having a garden."

"Oh, I love the garden," said Elsa.

"So did I," Eleanor said. After a moment she went on, "Hartley is very thoughtful, isn't he? He remembers as so few men do to bring home the books you want to read, flowers you love."

"He gave me this last week." Elsa leaned forward and pushed up the sleeve of her ivory silk blouse. "It's from

China." It was an old bracelet of twisted silver, set with a rough turquoise.

"Beautiful!" Eleanor said, smiling. "And don't you find he is fun to be with? He takes pains to tell a good story, to talk about things—so many men don't unless there are guests— and he is delightful to travel with. I remember—"

"Oh, we had such fun in Europe last summer," Elsa exclaimed eagerly. "We went poking into little French towns, and we went to Sicily. I'd always wanted to go to Sicily."

"I've never been there," said Eleanor. "You see, I live a very busy, restricted life."

"Do you?" Elsa's tone was wondering. "Why, somehow I thought of you as so—so gay—all sorts of parties—"

"No," said Eleanor. "No. I work nearly all the time. It's not easy to go to parties and work at the same time."

"Do you have to work?"

"I want to," said Eleanor. "Besides, I have my living to make."

Elsa said shyly, "Doesn't Hartley— Hartley would gladly— I know he would be glad to—"

"Oh, no," said Eleanor quickly. "I couldn't possibly take anything from Hartley."

Elsa opened her eyes very wide. "I mean," Eleanor went on, "I wouldn't be happy if I didn't earn my own living. As you say, each of us has a job. But I don't have many friends— almost none, in fact."

"I'd never have dreamed it," breathed Elsa. "Why, I have to have people—something going on—"

"No, we never know, do we? But I live an intensely lonely life. I work, eat, walk, sleep, alone. My evenings are practically all spent alone. Of course I know there are people I could invite, but why should I? They would come and then go, and I'd be as I was, alone. It's not only people that count— it's love and the person one loves and who loves in return."

The room was very still. Elsa was sitting motionless in her chair.

"It seems to me," Eleanor said, "that you must weigh your life. When you grow impatient, balance the sacrifices against the gains. Security, home, a garden, money, pretty clothes, all the people who want to know Mrs. Hartley Bainbridge, and, above all, love and your own house—it's pretty high pay for a job that, after all, isn't twenty-four hours a day. And there isn't much place in life, still, for the lonely woman. People are a little afraid of us, Elsa. We make too many women at the party."

Elsa brought her eyes to Eleanor's. "Are you sorry you aren't me?" she asked directly.

"No," Eleanor said slowly. "No. I'm— I made my choice. But you haven't the same reason, have you? You haven't a job you have to do, have you?"

Elsa shook her head. "I suppose not," she said.

"Leave me out of it," said Eleanor. "I'm a freak, let's say. But you're not. And honestly, if you don't hate Hartley, could you find a better job?"

Elsa was still looking at her. "No," she said honestly. "And certainly I don't hate him."

"No," agreed Eleanor. "If you went into an office, you'd have to mind your boss's little ways instead of Hartley's. None of us is free—wherever you are you have a boss. And if you're the boss it's even worse, because you know what the people under you are thinking."

"I've been silly," said Elsa.

"I like you," said Eleanor. "Hartley is lucky."

"I rather think I'm lucky, too," said Elsa.

"I think so," said Eleanor.

"I'll be going along." Elsa rose and tugged on the blue hat. "There! And thanks a lot!"

"Not at all," Eleanor replied.

They shook hands and walked to the door. Eleanor pressed the button. They waited in silence. But when the elevator was rushing up the shaft, Elsa bent suddenly and kissed Eleanor's cheek.

"I wish you weren't lonely," she whispered.

"Oh, I work very hard," Eleanor said, smiling. "I haven't much time for myself."

The elevator came, opened, and took her away. Eleanor went, smiling faintly, to take off her things. Before the mirror in her own room she looked at herself. She looked much older than—than she used to do. She'd been working too hard. Why? People didn't work like that unless they were sorrow-driven, Kurt had said one day. She had shaken her head. "I'm not driven," she said. "I'm doing what I like." Why, then, was there this ache in her throat, in her breast, in her heart?

Upon her cheek she could still feel the faint fresh imprint of the kiss which Hartley's wife had given her. She took her handkerchief and rubbed it away.

She woke next morning to a sense of disaster brought from yesterday. The sun was warm across her bed, but she felt weighted. She got up at once. There was nothing wrong. Everything was right. She had sent Elsa back to Hartley. Her play was finished—the dress rehearsal was this afternoon. She was looking forward to it. It was a good day, she told herself resolutely. She was going to start work on a new story. Perhaps she'd make Elsa the heroine of it. She knew what the heroine was inside, but she hadn't yet decided about the way she must look. And then maybe she'd have lunch out. And she'd promised to be at the theater early to look at some costumes. It was a nice full day. And so then, she asked herself over her pretty breakfast table, why did she feel something empty in it?

"Mattie," she said, her eyes on her newspaper, "when did Mr. Stenson call last?"

"Law, lemme see," said Mattie. "It ain't been for a week, I reckon."

"He didn't say anything about going away?"

"Naw'm, he just say, 'Is she all right?' And I say—"

"I'll probably hear from him," she said tranquilly.

It was ridiculous, after all she had said to Kurt, to feel emptiness because he let her alone. She must get to work. But
the story which she had thought was ready to be put down
did not come. She usually wrote swiftly and steadily, with
little correction. But today she scratched out line after line.
Her people did not move. They stood about, looking at her,
waiting for her to put her life into them, and she could not.
She shut her book impatiently at last. She needed a rest. She'd
not try now. When the play was opened, she'd go away
somewhere.

"Has any mail come, Mattie?" she called, ready to go out
for luncheon.

"Naw'm!" Mattie screamed from the kitchen.

Very well, she thought. She was absurd. She ate her luncheon and went to the theater and up to the costume room.

"I've come to look at those dresses, Mrs. Johnson," she told
the head sewing woman. Mrs. Johnson hurried forward. She
had once been rather a good actress. But she looked, with
her gray stiff hair and black apron and pricked rough fingers,
as though she had lived all her life among stuffs.

"Yes, Miss Dane. You see, the sketch says, 'A red material,
taffeta or a stiff silk.' Now, do you think this red is— Of course,
it's late, but I could dye it a little off of the scarlet—"

Eleanor held up the flaming scarlet gown. "No, scarlet is
what I'd thought."

"Yes, but it's to go with this blue. You see, the other girl
wears blue. And oh, Miss Dane, is this what they mean by a
penguin dress for the old lady?"

Eleanor was heaped about with the garments of her people.
It was strange, when she had always woven their garments
out of words, to find herself now handling tangible materials,
looking at colors to be seen. She felt the shock of actual flesh
and blood, as though her people had come out of her book
and demanded human frame. She forgot for a while everything else.

When it was finished, she looked at her watch and discovered that the rehearsal had already begun. She could not enter the theater from the stage. Instead she must go downstairs, through the winding basements and through a side door. She fumbled her way between pipes and furnaces, over uneven bricked floors, up the janitor's winding stair, into the theater. The stage burst upon her, coming out of the dusty under-darkness. It was brilliant with costume and light.

"Play that up—play that up!" Mr. Bredon was roaring to a girl in a blue gown. "Don't you see? In a moment she's coming in—the girl you wish you were, the girl more beautiful than you, more brilliant, a girl in a red gown!"

Eleanor sat down quickly, entranced. She was glad the theater was empty for this first time she saw her play really finished. Without the costumes the actors had still been not quite her people. But now—she leaned forward. The emptiness which had haunted the day was almost filled.

The play marched on. It was good—it was good! Now she began to wish for the audience. The turns of wit she had tucked in slyly here and there—Mrs. Brace in her black satin— was Mrs. Brace as funny as she thought she had made her? The first act drew near its close. Mrs. Brace had the two girls in hand then. The curtain ought to go down on an audience stamping and roaring with laughter. It would be hard to judge from these rows of empty seats. How she'd argued with Bredon over that last speech of Mrs. Brace's!

"You've got to make that crack plainer," Bredon had said. "You have to have things print plain for the average theater mob."

"It's my way to say things just under what I mean," Eleanor had insisted. "It's just what Mrs. Penguin would say."

In the end they had decided to leave it to the crowd. If on the first night they laughed, she was right. If they didn't, she must change it. In the darkness of the empty theater she waited anxiously for the moment. Bredon, waiting too, turned toward her significantly. Mrs. Brace—she always thought of her as Mrs. Brace—came in on her cue. "In my opinion, girls—" her speech began. Eleanor listened. Was it funny or not? She had heard it so often she couldn't tell. There—that was the end. Tomorrow night—

But out of the empty theater came a great burst of laughter, a roar of laughter, a shout, echoing among the galleries. They all stared, startled, into the shadows. What laughter! Who could—

"What the devil!" shouted Bredon.

Eleanor rose. Nobody on earth had such a laugh as that except Kurt. None but he could shake a building with his laughter.

"Kurt!" she cried into the darkness. She ran down the aisle. "Kurt, where are you?"

He stood up, tall and dim, in the far end of the theater, out of a wilderness of empty seats.

"Here, my Eleanor," he called to her. He began striding over the seats like a long-legged Titan, and he met her in the aisle. On the stage the curtain had fallen and there was the bustle of changing scenery. No one paid any heed to them. Bredon smiled at her. "You got your laugh tonight anyway, Miss Dane!" he called, and hurried to the next act.

"Kurt!" she demanded. He was holding both her hands. "What are you doing here? Why aren't you on the expedition?" Now that she had found him, safe and alive and exactly the same, she could be angry at him. Now that he had not gone, she could be angry with him because he had not gone, angry because he was here again, because she had been empty without him.

"I came to see your play," he said cheerfully. His eyes were shining.

"I called you up," she said, and decided that she would not say she had gone to his house. He might think—

"Ah, I am just for now in my club," he said. "Lars, he had the cable from his old father he was about to die, and I gave him holiday for it. Let us sit down. It is a wonderful play, my Eleanor. I so honor the great gift in you."

"Don't put me off, Kurt," she said severely. "Why didn't you go on the expedition?"

"Hush!" he whispered loudly. "The curtain goes up!"

She watched him and he watched the play. He laughed, he listened, he slapped his knee and laughed again. He forgot her entirely. Between the scenes he was talking to Bredon, talking to the actors, impatient for the curtain. In the last act she watched his face grow tense. Laughter was over now. The girl in the blue dress must die in this last act. Not even Mrs. Brace could keep her alive. The play was a skillful tragedy. People would laugh and laugh until suddenly they found themselves crying. The final curtain went down. Kurt, staring, his arms folded on the seat ahead of him, gave a gusty sigh.

"Ah, yes," he sighed. "It's right—life is so. She had to die, the little piteous creature—but she had to die." He rose, fumbling for his hat and gloves.

"Kurt!" she said. She felt herself so forgotten that she was half jealous of the creature she had made. She found herself saying, "Kurt, let's have dinner together!"

"Yes," he said, "yes!" He seemed quite dazed.

In the street she took his arm. "This way," she said. "Let's go to Monelli's. I don't feel like going home."

"I see she had to die," he said dolefully.

"It's only a play!" she cried to comfort him.

But he shook his head. "It's life," he said simply, and she was reproached. What she had valued as most precious in herself, he valued more than she. She was humbled by the value he set upon what she had done.

They dined in strange quiet in the little Italian restaurant. Kurt said almost nothing. Once he put out his hand and placed it upon hers.

"Such a gift!" he murmured. And he said again, "I bow before you, Eleanor!"

"Don't!" she cried in a low voice. By his praise he seemed to put her afar off. She didn't want to be far away. She wanted to be near him.

She pressed him again. "Why, why, Kurt, didn't you go on the expedition?"

He looked up, astonished. "And leave you?"

"Why not?" she asked, astonished in turn.

He looked at her gravely. "I see you still don't know how I love you," he said. "You still cannot comprehend love. I knew what the play meant to you."

"And I what the expedition was to you," she interrupted him.

His eyes twinkled suddenly. "The Himalayas are still there," he said. "But the play—it must come first."

"Kurt!" she whispered.

Light broke over her heart like a dawn. Love—the love of a man like Kurt—it was different! Love wasn't a thing in itself. It was what people made it. A great heart made love great.

He began to speak abruptly. "Now I shan't ask you to marry me any more," he was saying. "I have seen this great play. The books—I said to myself, 'She can write books anywhere. She shall have hours to write. I will ask nothing. But perhaps when she is weary she will come to me.' But now I have seen this play. And I know there must be more plays. I will not ask you any more to marry me, my darling. But I am here forever. There is never another for me except you. I love you. I love you so much that I want you to have your own life as you will have it."

He was leaning across the table. She was staring at him.

"But, Kurt," she said, "your own work—"

"I will do that," he said. "But it is not so great as your work. I discover, but I cannot create. I will go away alone sometimes and do my work, and I will come back to you. But I will never ask you to come with me. Only let me sometimes come back to you."

She looked away from him. "I feel," she said, her lips beginning to quiver, "I feel as though you were saying goodbye."

"No, never!" he exclaimed. "Why do you feel so, my Eleanor?"

"I don't know," she said. She took out her handkerchief and wiped her eyes. "I don't know what I want, Kurt! I don't know how to choose!"

He moved his chair to draw near her, to shield her from the others. "You don't have to choose," he said. "There is no choice to be made, Eleanor. Your life goes on as you have made it, and I am always the same, loving you. You shall not be disturbed."

Her life would go on the same, he said. That was what she had wanted—just to go on as she was. And she could go on, and he would never change, he said. Then why was it the thought of her living room frightened her? She was desperately tired, but if she laid herself down in her lonely bed it would not be to sleep.

He put out his hand gently, saying nothing, and took her hand, lying lax in her lap. Her hand lay enfolded, and she let it lie. And then, slowly, the touch told her. His hand, holding her hand so gently, without possession, without demand, told her. She could not live without him. She could not even do her work without the completion he could give her. And he would never again ask her to marry him.

"Kurt," she said, looking up quickly to him, "will you marry me?"

A brilliant red rushed into his face, his eyes widened, he dropped her hand and drew his chair back quickly.

"What—what—?" he stammered.

"Will you marry me, Kurt?" she said again. Relief poured into her, an instant peace. Of course! For how could she let a love like this escape her?

"Take care, Eleanor!" he exclaimed. "Take care what you say!"

She shook her head and smiled. "Please marry me, Kurt!"

"I don't know," he said in agitation. "I am—I didn't expect

it. It's too—quick. I've been—arranging myself all these months to—to live without it. It's— Can I dare to do it? I don't know."

She could scarcely believe this was he, so shy, so doubtful. Why, Kurt was trembling!

"But I dare," she said.

They looked at each other. Suddenly she laughed. "Oh, Kurt, think! Here I am, teasing you, begging you, cajoling you—to marry me! And you won't!"

He wavered an instant, and then out came his great roar of laughter to meet her laughter.

"Waiter," he shouted, "the bill!" He leaped to his feet. "We will go home," he declared, "where I can kiss you! So!"

They were married immediately. For why should they wait? Her mind and heart were empty of everything now except the immense inexpressible joy of finding Kurt.

She had a moment or two of old fear. That first morning in Kurt's small house, when she came in to breakfast the habit of old fear fell on her. Did he like her as well as love her? Hartley had loved her, but he hadn't liked the person she really was. He had wanted her to be someone else. But Kurt's warm uncritical eyes welcomed her.

"How do you like your eggs, Eleanor?" he asked.

"How do you have yours?" she parried.

"That has nothing to do with you," he retorted.

"Then I don't want any eggs at all," she said. "Only fruit and toast and coffee."

He uncovered a dish of toast and poured coffee for her and helped himself largely to eggs.

"So!" he said. "We each have what we like. And now, my Eleanor, we will plan."

They planned together, and he did not run ahead of her. He divined the old timid habit in her and delicately he drew her on. She found herself saying, "I've always wanted to see a fjord."

"Why not?" he said. "We will go."

"And I want to see a Swedish farm," she said happily. She had forgotten there was so much she wanted.

"Ah, that's where my mother is waiting!" he exclaimed.

Weeks later, across the sea on that Swedish farm, it was his small wrinkled independent mother, she decided, who had given Kurt this valuation of a woman. For he was not deferent to her as his wife, and she had received deference as a woman. He was, indeed, quite ruthless. He let her struggle with a window, he did not pull out her chair. "Why should I do these thing when you can do them?" he said. Hartley had leaped to do such things for her and then he had bound her soul.

But Kurt left her free to struggle and to be. When she said in the little hotel by the fjord in Norway, "I'd like to stay a day or two," he said, "Stay, then, my Eleanor. Why not?" He left her and went on his own business to Stockholm, and when she could not bear being away from him she joined him there. She was not sure that there was no pique in her.

"Didn't you miss me?" she demanded of him.

"Horribly," he said. "But I didn't want to stay any more there."

"Why didn't you tell me?" she asked.

"What had it to do with you, if you wanted to stay?" he replied calmly.

She preceived that this was to be a marriage of independence and was troubled. For could marriage be so independent?

"Shall we not stay away from each other too long sometimes?" she asked doubtfully.

"Time will show us," he answered. "If we wish to do so, let us do it." So day by day together they explored their marriage.

He said one July morning, "I feel ready now for the Himalayas. I have my materials ready, and the season is good."

She said, "Shall I go with you?"

He said, "I don't know. What do you want to do?"

And she looked at him in the fullness of love. "If you had said, 'Yes,' I might have drawn back. Being so free, I know I want to go this time with you."

"We will never decide beyond each time as it comes," he said serenely.

He was so serene that she was driven by curiosity to ask of that serenity, "What would you have done if I had said I didn't want to go?"

"I would have gone, missing you horribly, but wanting most for you to be what you are."

"If I had asked you to stay?" she persisted.

"Oh, no, Eleanor," he said quickly. "I can't imagine it."

"But if I had?"

"I should have gone," he said gently, "trusting you to want me to be what I am."

She said no more. Here was marriage, a rock beneath her, a roof over her head, a sky above. She ceased all questioning and accepted the days with joy.

"Goodbye, Mother," she said to Kurt's mother.

"Goodbye, goodbye," the old woman said gaily from her doorstep.

"She's a good sport, Kurt," she said. "Some mothers would have minded goodbye."

"Not she," Kurt said proudly. "It's her way to send her sons onward with good cheer. She wants us to be what our souls demand."

In this large atmosphere Eleanor now lived. The immensity of the earth over which they sped by plane and ship was not larger than the freedom in which she lived with Kurt. When they crossed India to the foothills of the Himalayas, they were not strange, those huge uplifted hoary heads. She was not dwarfed by anything now, being so free.

"Siva," Kurt said, "Siva, the great god, meditates in those mountains, his matted locks white with age." And after a day or two in the small clean hotel kept by a black-skinned white-turbaned Indian proprietor, Kurt went out and brought back the cream-white pony of her dreams.

"I knew he was waiting for you," Kurt said, laughing.

The cream-white pony carried her beside his brown one up those first green slopes, up until the river was a silver stream, up through the rain forests of great oaks, their roots ferny, their branches dripping gray moss, their trunks wrapped in thick vines. Up, up they went—past silver fir and birch, then beyond the trees into the snows and over the frozen streams. There had been shepherds on the flowery lower grasslands, but here there were none. Above and beyond stretched still higher against the sky ten thousand snowy peaks. There was that first evening upon the snows, and the sun sank among the peaks, scarlet and gold. They pitched their tents and slept, and in the night they woke and stole out, in the bottomless silence, to see the full moon swinging over the ramparts of the mountains. And they rose at dawn to see the sun fling up its rays. She had never lived in such intensity of sun and moon and mountains. In such intensity she lived with Kurt as day followed day and they ascended each day nearer to the tops of the snowy peaks.

And as she ascended, a certain dream took stronger hold on her. When they had lingered in the green and flower-starred foothills, she had said to him one day, suddenly, as the wish flew out of her heart, "I wish I could find your flower."

Kurt had shaken his head. "It's not in the foothills, Eleanor. It grows very high up in the snows. It may be you will not want to go so far with me."

She had not answered. But in herself she had determined she would go as far as he did. When at last the ponies could climb no farther on the glaciers, and the packs must be put upon the shoulders of mountain coolies, she said nothing. Kurt looked at her with question, but she only smiled. If he could climb, so could she—so could she! She struggled upward, breathless with the rare atmosphere, always, however weary, watching for the glint of sudden blue. She searched for it continually, her eyes running hither and thither as they climbed.

And then, one day, she found it. They had come out of their tent at dawn, after a night's encampment. There had been many flowers in the patches of snow and bare rock below the glacier, rhododendrons, red and pink and lavender, mauve primulas, crimson strawberry flowers, iris and anemone, blue wild delphinium and dwarfed white lilacs upon dark rocks. But none of these was Kurt's flower. Now here in a dawn it was growing at her feet. She had looked down, half in habit, and there it was, deep blue against the snows.

"Kurt!" she cried. "Look! Here at my feet!"

He dropped to his knees and with his bare hands he brushed away the snow.

"The flower!" he whispered. "You have found it for me!"

. . . She would never forget it, she thought in the evening of that day, gazing into the upper mountains.

A carrier had that afternoon brought them mail from the last post, where they had left the ponies. She tore open the letter with the American stamp and unfolded a large square sheet of paper and read. Kurt was watching her. She could feel his gaze upon her face.

"Bredon says the play is still running," she said. "He's going to carry it over into the next season. He wants the new play— as soon as I'm ready."

"Good!" Kurt said. "And now, what is in your heart, my Eleanor? Shall we go back? Are you ready?"

They stood looking upward into the range upon range of snow-covered mountains. She felt so light, so free. Kurt had set her feet upon the path of freedom. She had begun it alone, but now he went with her. She was another woman still. Now this was she, complete in joy upon these mountains.

"I don't want to go back," she whispered. He put his arm around her. "Not yet, Kurt! I'll tell you when I'm ready!"

Yes, she could tell him and trust him. At the hour when she said, "I want to go back to my own work," they would go back. He understood her. And she could say it with ease, the flower being found. It was growing now, this moment, in its box, transplanted from the snow. They would keep it alive.

Her heart was tight with joy. What was that old Eastern story Kurt was telling her of the man who feared his heart might burst with joy and so he bound it with a silver band? She turned to Kurt and smiled.

"Put a band about my heart, too, Kurt. I feel it might burst with joy this moment!"

But he shook his head and bent to kiss her.

"No bands, my darling! Love binds with no bands!" he said.

John-John Chinaman

Young John Lim paused in his ironing of the mayor's dress shirt and looked at the clock. It was five minutes to four and the hours of peace were gone. In a few minutes the street, the wide street of a small Midwestern American town, would be full of children and among them the savage boys. How he hated them! They had tortured his own childhood.

He too had gone to the red brick school half a block away from his father's laundry. The mornings he had managed by being as late as he dared, and his teachers, eyeing him sternly through the grades, grew tolerant of him as one by one they found out that he was always easily the head of his class. He would have been the valedictorian had the faculty not felt that the tie between him and Jim Halley, the principal's son, was so close that Jim ought to have it. "After all, Jim's an American," people said.

John Lim had come home to his father that day to weep the angry tears of the Chinese boy who is not taught that a man does not cry.

"Did you not tell me I was born in America?" he asked his father in their angular Cantonese dialect.

"You were born in the great city of St. Louis," Mr. Lim replied.

"Am I not American?" John demanded again.

"According to the laws of this country, you are American," Mr. Lim replied. Then he said sadly, "But the hearts of people decide these things, not laws."

"John-John Chinaman, eat dead rat—" At that very moment their voices hooting the rude song came in through the window.

"Why did you name me John, Father?" he had asked.

"The first white man I ever knew was a good man who was named John," Mr. Lim said, "and he gave me food when I had none and helped me when I was ill, and I swore my first son should be named John." Mr. Lim had not stopped his ironing.

John had learned after a while to imitate his father and, in spite of his wrath, to go on ironing and never to lift his eyes. But today he could not.

Ever since Siu-lan, his little wife, had come, this torture had made his hatred flame with new anger. Was it not torture? Yes, he understood her fear. All during his childhood he had been afraid. He had had to pick up dead mice the white children had thrown into the laundry, sometimes into the clean clothes. He had had to scrub chalk marks from the door, crazy imitations of Chinese characters. At night the doorbell might ring and there was always the possibility that a customer might be there out of hours, though more often there was only a jeer of laughter from around the corner. In the summer idle boys came to tease and whistle through their fingers and make fun at the open door, and when the door was shut the little room with two irons going became hot beyond bearing.

Sometimes since he left school he had not been able to

endure, and then he had rushed out at the boys with his iron and scattered them. But the boys were only delighted to have so roused him, and they were soon back.

"We are the foreigners here," his father had told him one day, the sweat pouring down his bare back. "In our country we think the white man the foreigner. I remember that once a white man came through our village. We all ran away across the fields, men, women, and children together, because he seemed to us so fearful and strange."

John had answered through clenched teeth, "But I am American as much as anyone else is."

"Ah," his father had said enigmatically without looking up, "what is an American? I often wonder."

Now he heard soft quick footsteps on the stairs and he looked up and saw her, his little wife, a small terrified child in her long Chinese robe. She ran past him to the window and stood hiding behind the curtain, staring out into the street.

"They are coming!" she whispered. "I am afraid."

She drew back from the open window and a shrill yell rose up from the building down the street. He was horrified to see the delicate color drain from her face until it was like creamy wax. He ran to her side, leaving the iron on the bosom of the mayor's good shirt. "Don't be afraid!" he said. "See, it's only the bad boys!"

Upon the closed door there were thumps and raps, and through it they heard the same rhyme that he had so loathed in his childhood.

"John-John Chinaman, eat dead rat—"

"At least they might make up a new one," he thought in his raging heart.

"Oh, hear—they even cry your own name!" Siu-lan gasped.

Before he could explain, a small stone flew in through the window and struck his head just above the temple. Then she screamed and he could do nothing to calm her. Blood was flowing down his cheek.

"Why do they hate us so?" she was crying. "What have we ever done? Oh, let us go home and never come here again!"

He had to find a cloth to wipe his head lest the blood stain her pretty silk gown, and she followed him. It was at this moment that they smelled the burning.

"Now they have set the house on fire!" she whispered.

But he knew the smell of burning linen and he fled to lift the iron and yet not in time to be before his father, who at this moment was already at the door. It was too late. On the shirt bosom was a brown burn.

Mr. Lim looked at his son. "It is the mayor's good shirt," he said severely.

"I know it," John said. "How I could have been so stupid!" He paused and bit his lip. "But she was afraid and I went to her."

"There is a point beyond which it is unfilial to love one's wife," Mr. Lim said. Then he laughed, seeing the small figure shrinking against the wall. "What shall I tell Mr. Bascom? Shall I say my son is so in love with his wife that he leaves the iron in the bosom of the mayor's only good shirt?"

John snatched the shirt out of his father's hand. "I will take it to him myself," he exclaimed. "I will tell him the truth— that she was so terrified by the rudeness of the boys in this city that I had to—had to—" He was suddenly unable to bear the twinkle he saw in his father's eye, and he rushed out with the shirt rolled under his arm.

At the very moment when he passed the school Mr. Halley, the principal, was coming out of his office. John stopped, an idea suddenly poised in his mind.

"Good evening, Mr. Halley," he said.

Mr. Halley looked around. He was a tall sandy man, all of a color, and that the color of Median dust. There was nothing to set him apart from any other man in Median, but John knew every line of his face and figure. He was more than the principal of the high school—he was Jim's father, and

Jim had been one of the torturers, almost until he was the valedictorian.

"Oh—hello, John," Mr. Halley said. His key, for some reason, stuck in the lock—he must see about a new one.

John sprang forward. "Allow me, please," he said. With his delicate yellow fingers he manipulated the key and it turned.

"Why, thank you, John," Mr. Halley said. He was ready to go on when he became aware of a slight quivering upon the smooth young Chinese face.

"I hope your son Jim is well?" John said urgently.

Mr. Halley was touched. Jim was his only son. "Why, that's mighty nice of you, John," he said cordially. "Jim is getting on just fine. He graduates this June from the state university, and if I do say it myself, he's done well. I'm proud of him and so is his mother."

"Yes, sir," John said. He was preparing Mr. Halley for his idea and now, seeing the mellow look on the sandy face, he plunged ahead, knowing that Americans are not to be held long in one place.

"Mr. Halley, sir," he said very fast, "you are so kind, please let me ask you one thing. I am just married and a young wife new come from a village near Canton, China, is naturally strange here."

When he tried to speak correct English without using the easy slang of the street, he grew suddenly Chinese and could scarcely speak at all. But he forced on.

"The boys, sir, frighten her very much. They shout and sing bad things at our house, and sometimes throw in dead rats, and today a stone hit me before her eyes." He pointed diffidently toward his temple. "She thinks, sir, they do these things to express hatred to us, and she is frightened to step from our door. She wishes to return to China."

Mr. Halley clucked his tongue. "Well now, certainly they mustn't throw stones. I'll speak to them about that. I am sorry, John. But as for the rest of it—well, you know how boys are.

You've lived here a long time, haven't you?"

"All my life," John murmured.

Mr. Halley took his watch out of his pocket. His wife would be expecting him early because this was prayer-meeting night.

"Yes, well," he said, "you must tell your little wife not to be afraid, John. Married, are you? Well, I guess Jim will be marrying one of these days. I'll certainly tell the boys not to throw any more stones." He smiled kindly, made a signal of farewell with his hand raised and dropped, and hurried down the street.

So John went on to the square that was in the middle of Median, and up the tree-shaded brick walk to the brick building that was the pride of the town. He went doggedly up the steps and toward the mayor's office. Everybody went into that office unannounced and so did he, and there he found the mayor sitting with his coat off in the early heat of May. He was in a welter of papers which he was signing while a young woman with an ugly face waited at his elbow. He glanced up when the door opened.

"Hello, John," he said.

"How do you do, Mr. Mayor?" John replied.

"Sit down," the mayor said. John sat down carefully sidewise on a small chair. Although the mayor did not know it, this was the way citizens in China were taught to sit in the presence of those above them.

The mayor did not look up from the papers again, nor did he stop his flying pen, scrawling "Jonathan P. Bascom" over and over as fast as he could.

"What can I do for you, John?" he asked.

The mayor always insisted that he liked his Chinese. The Lim family were law-abiding decent people and they made good citizens, though of course, he always added, "They're different from us."

John took the shirt slowly from under his arm and spread it on the desk. The mayor looked up and saw the brown mark shaped like an iron bottom in the middle of his shirt.

"What the hell!" he said simply, and put down his pen.

"Mr. Mayor, sir," John said, "this is your good shirt."

"I see it is," the mayor said.

"I burned it," John said quickly, "and, Mr. Mayor, sir, please allow me to tell you first how it happened."

"That shirt cost me four good dollars," the mayor remarked.

John's too sensitive soul shrank from the implication.

"Mr. Mayor, sir, we pay for the shirt, my father and I. It is not to avoid the payment that I wish to explain. It is the situation how it was burned."

"All right." He raised his pale bushy eyebrows at the ugly young woman. "Come back in five minutes, Louise," he said. The mayor never told anyone who came into his office how long he could stay, but he always told Louise when to come back and everybody knew what he meant.

"I will not take so long," John said. The door had not closed behind the girl before he was pouring out the story of his tortured childhood.

"Sir, I feared the end of school. How I planned every day I would run like hell, sir! As soon as the teacher said, 'School dismissed,' I had my books under my arm and I ran down the street so fast like hell. Then I hid in our house, not daring to come out until night, and sometimes dead rats to throw out, and sometimes dirty water in the window on the clothes. Not always, sir, but who knows when? My father said, 'Never mind, these are only the children,' but where would the children have learned except from their parents? Besides, sir, I also was a child, and I had no other playmates. I used to think, 'Why do they hate me who never did them any harm? I am born in America, too.' "

The mayor leaned his elbows on his papers. He listened because he always listened to anyone who wanted to talk to him, but at this moment it was hard to take in just what this young Chinese was saying. The question raging in his mind was, could it be possible that fellow in the White House was really going to lead the country into war? He had been riding at his breakneck speed over the Kansas roads only the day before and had drawn up under a tree and, sitting there alone, had turned on his radio and listened to the President speaking.

"All continents may become involved in a worldwide war," the voice of the President had said.

At this the mayor had turned the radio off and had sat with the tears streaming down his cheeks like any old woman. He was glad he was alone because he had never told anyone exactly what he had gone through years ago when he was young and in France. It had been impossible even to tell his wife. How could a good woman who had always lived in a little peaceful town like Median know what war was, and how men behaved in war?

Then he had jammed in his gears. "I'm going to fight like hell to keep us out of war," he had roared to the Kansas landscape.

These letters piled on his desk were part of that fight. Now he looked across them and a general notion of what John was talking about pierced to his mind.

"Mighty sorry, John," he said vaguely. The door opened and Louise came back. "Don't bother about the shirt," he said. He took his pen and began writing his name furiously. "Nice of you to come in, John," he said. It was his way of saying goodbye, and John rose.

"Certainly we will pay for the shirt, sir," he said proudly, and went away.

Had the mayor heard or had he not heard? John asked himself. Only time could tell. When he reached home he went in and nodded to his father and before he said anything else he asked.

"Where is she?"

"In the kitchen," his father replied. He was just finishing ironing a dress and was edging its ruffles delicately. "Was the mayor angry?" he called after his son.

"No," John said without turning.

"A good man, our mayor," Mr. Lim thought, holding up the dress and slipping in onto a hanger. He glanced at his son's back and a sly merriment lightened his small, somewhat sad eyes. Six months ago he had called his son into his room and put before him the photographs he had been given by a Chinese matchmaker in St. Louis. This he had done with his usual calm and benign manner, taking it for granted that his only son would agree with him in the wisdom of a wife from Canton rather than one of the bold Americanized daughters of his friends in St. Louis. The house needed a woman. His son's mother had died five years ago and Mr. Lim himself had no wish to marry again. His elder cousin who lived with them was too old, and his still older uncle, who had first owned this laundry, was now bed-ridden upstairs. Obviously, John must marry.

But Mr. Lim had been kind. He had allowed John to decide which one he liked best among the round innocent childlike faces of the matchmaker's photographs.

John had stared down at the one held in his hand. "But with a wife from Canton, Father, what would I talk about?" he had asked. The face in the little glossy picture was so childish and soft!

Mr. Lim had looked at John over his brass-rimmed spectacles as severely as he was ever able to look.

"Silence in a wife is better than talk," he had said. "Your mother soothed me by her silence."

John had put down the photograph. "What if I don't like her?"

"If you do not like your fiancée when she comes, you need not marry her," Mr. Lim had said, watching him. Being born in America put something strangely rebellious into Chinese sons!

"I should say not," John had said.

Mr. Lim smiled now as he remembered and he took up old Dr. Lane's nightshirt. "She is already in his heart," he thought.

In the kitchen John was lighting the gas range for his little wife. He had taught her how to light it, but she was still afraid and had waited for him.

Now she cried in her pretty voice, "Oh, how I am glad you have come—are you safe?"

He laughed and blew out the match. "Do not be afraid any more," he said. "I went to see the mayor and I told him about the boys."

"What is a mayor?" she asked, her eyes still anxious.

"It is like the magistrate in your father's village," John replied.

Her look changed, incredulous and proud. "Oh," she breathed, "and you could speak to him?"

He nodded and then she flushed delicately.

"Oh," she said again and then made a great effort and went on. "Dolling!" she said faintly.

It was a name he had been trying to teach her for days. But he had made the mistake of first explaining to her what it meant and then she had been too shy to speak it. Her little face was now instantly as red as a peony, for this word had certainly not been among the things her mother had taught her should be said to a husband. But her face was not visible for more than one second. The next second it was buried in young John's shoulder. He had his arms around her again.

"What if I hadn't chosen her picture!" he thought in a panic. But he had—he had!

. . . "Here's your letter from the mayor, John," Bill Peters, the postman, said. Although he had known Mr. Lim for twenty years, he still did not know his name was not John.

Mr. Lim took the letter with both hands, as one receives an official document in China. He felt a shiver of fear. Had his rebellious son been disrespectful to the mayor?

"Thank you, sir, Mr. Peters," he said, and then went into a cubbyhole under the stairs where he kept pickles and salt fish and small stocks of dried foods from Canton. There in privacy he read the letter. He could not understand what the mayor was talking about, so he read it again. Certainly the letter spoke about his son, but it also spoke about war. " 'Our sons are not again to be sacrificed on foreign soil to preserve foreign imperialisms,' " he read aloud very slowly.

"I must look in the dictionary," he thought, so he took the letter up into the room which he shared with the two old men who spent most of their time in bed, and there by the square table he worked out what the mayor said. Foreign imperialisms meant what Japan was at this moment doing to China. Every Chinese knew what evil that was. But foreign soil? This was not so clear. He decided to consult the two old men, for he had been taught to believe in the wisdom of his elders.

Begging their pardon for awakening them, Mr. Lim explained the letter in Cantonese as well as he could, and the uncle listened carefully, and the cousin, too. Both were withered little old men with sparse white beards, and age had turned them almost into twins. Had it not been for the war, they would by now have gone back to China to die and be buried. As it was, they were trying to outlive the war.

"There is to be a war here also, that I can see for myself," Mr. Lim said, "but by whom and for what reason I cannot tell."

"It is Japan, be certain," the old uncle said. "Japan makes war on the whole world and causes inconvenience to us all."

"The mayor does not say Japan," Mr. Lim said, examining the letter again.

"A wise man does not always say what he means," the cousin murmured.

"He says our sons are not to be sacrificed on foreign soil," Mr. Lim said.

"So far, it is good," the old uncle said.

"He says foreign empires are not to be preserved."

"That, too, is good," the old uncle said.

The three elderly men looked at each other.

"That is the heart of the letter," Mr. Lim said.

"Then tell the mayor we agree to it," said the old uncle, who as the eldest was technically the head of the family.

Mr. Lim went back to his ironing and wondered why he still felt confused, and when his son came downstairs he took the letter out of his bosom and handed it to him.

"A letter from the mayor," he said. "See if you know its purpose."

John read it quickly. The words which his father had searched for in the dictionary were not hard for him. As he read them, certain things he had been taught in school came back to him. The Salute to the American Flag, the Declaration of Independence, "The Star-Spangled Banner," "My Country 'Tis of Thee," the birthdays of Washington and Lincoln, all these had something to do with this letter—patriotism, in a word! He laughed at it. What was there for him to fight for in a small dusty town whose citizens' clothes he washed and whose children had made his life hateful with their cruelties! This America!

He handed the letter back to his father. "You have always taught me that only the lowest of men become soldiers," he said. He quoted a Chinese proverb glibly, "Poor iron for nails, poor men for soldiers."

"That is true," Mr. Lim said calmly. "It is why China has never made a game of war. We despise war. On the other hand, there are robbers and thieves among nations as among men. Do you forget Japan and our own country?"

"What have I to do with that? I am an American," John said coolly.

Mr. Lim did not answer this too shrewd remark. He folded Mrs. Bascom's full petticoat with the expertness of years.

"Doubtless the mayor will tell us what he means," he said diplomatically. To himself he thought again that it was not easy for a Chinese to be the father of an American son. There was something about this country stronger than race or training. When a man was born here, a spirit was born in him that did not come from his two parents. What would his grandson be?

As for John, he began to work in silence and the American ferment in him said angrily that he would fight no wars for a country whose citizens treated him like yellow scum. So that even children kept his beautiful little wife in constant terror. If, as now appeared likely, she was going to have a child, could he bear to bring up his son as he himself had had to grow up?

"There must be something better to fight for here than the white race before I fight," he thought grimly.

. . . The mayor's letters worked like yeast in Median. There were some people for and some against them, but the Lims said nothing and did nothing, old Mr. Lim because he was thinking of many things and John because he was thinking of only the one thing—that he owed nothing to America. Meanwhile the laundry work went on, heavy with wash dresses and shirts. Summer came and school was out and the days were here that John dreaded. Idle boys, mischievous boys, a few downright bad boys, and did no one see what they did? He kept hoping the mayor would speak to them—and had Mr. Halley forgotten?

The boys in their freedom tortured the Chinese whenever they thought of it, on their way back and forth to the movies, to the swimming hole, anywhere. At the first shout, Siu-lan was flying upstairs—to stay, sometimes, until night grew late enough for peace. What could John do but rage until he could not eat? Mr. Lim could do nothing with him.

"You must try not to be frightened," Mr. Lim told his daughter-in-law one day when John was delivering clothes to old Mrs. Cole, who was an invalid. "He is too angry. Evil will come of it. The woman must be wise for the man."

"I will try," Siu-lan whispered piteously. She did try, but John saw through her at once.

"Do not pretend," he said fiercely. "I cannot bear it."

So she gave up pretending and the days went on unchanged.

Jim Halley came home, and once he passed John on the street.

"Hello, John," he said in the same careless way he had always spoken.

"Hello, Jim," John replied, careful to say no more.

He knew in the ways that everybody knew everything in this little town that Jim was the hero here this summer. When he came home the town had given him a big party, and the mayor had made a speech. "Median's honored young son," he had said of Jim, and then he had gone off to his favorite theme. He had called upon all parents of sons to consider the loss to the nation of such young men as Jim Halley. John had not been there. He had said he was too busy to go, but Mr. Lim, sitting on a narrow bench in the hot sun, had as usual listened carefully to the mayor's speech. The upshot of it, he decided, was that there was going to be a war and the nation would need its young men.

He took this thought home with him in quiet soberness.

"There is to be a war and all young men must go, mayor said today," he told his son at their evening meal.

"Not me," John said firmly. "I'm a married man."

Mr. Lim answered this by silence, and in silence the meal was finished. But upstairs that night John talked a great deal to his little wife.

"Do not think I would go to war even if I were not exempt," he told her. "I would renounce my citizenship first and go back to China."

At this she buried her head under his arm. "It is true the stove is better here than there," she said.

He pulled her out. "And do you not hate these boys as you did?"

To which she replied, "I dare not go out when they come, but now I notice also there are days they do not come. And I like very much the way the water flows out of the wall, hot and cold. In our village the bucket was small and the well deep, and my arms ached so at night that sometimes I could not sleep."

He fixed her with a sternly loving gaze.

"Do you like America?" he asked her.

"I do like America," she said honestly. "It is only the people—why do they not like us? It would be a good country if they liked us."

He shook his head. "You ask me what I cannot answer," he said. "I hate them," he added simply.

For though there are whole days and even weeks when they lived peacefully, yet there was no telling when suddenly there would be an outbreak of trouble, as for instance one morning in August when a loud harsh tapping came apparently from the outer wall. It was John who discovered at last a small metal toy stuck to the wall with a string tied to it, and at the end of the string a boy. John threw the thing at him and cut the boy's cheek and stood scowling while he ran home.

In a little while Hen Conolly, the garage mechanic, came to bang on the laundry door, and when John opened it the angry Irishman wanted to know what the hell John meant by hitting his boy on the cheek with a tick-tack-toe.

"What the hell does your son mean to put such a thing on my house?" John retorted and shut the door in his face.

Mr. Lim heard Hen's loud voice shouting in the street, "It's time these Chinks went back where they came from!"

"You should not have angered him," Mr. Lim said.

"He should not have angered *me*," John retorted. "I'm as good as he is."

Mr. Lim was silent. This, he perceived, was the American thing in John, and he sighed.

In October it became apparent to Median that their young men must register for the army and if there were to be a war they would have to go. The mayor banged the table in the city hall and shouted.

"Damn it, if I have to send our boys to war I'm going to do it fighting! We're going to have the biggest protest meeting we've ever had the day the draft is drawn, and the first boy drafted is goin' to get a purse of money and a guarantee of the best job in the city when he gets back! He's going to get paid to do the dirtiest work in the world, and don't you think money is enough! He's goin' to get our highest honor and all we can give him! He's goin' as the first American of our town. For when a young man gives himself to the country, he gives something that can't be made up to him."

The mayor's eyes were suddenly hot with tears again. He was seeing another young man, himself, marching out of Median to another war, and nothing had made up to him for those years when he had had to kill his fellow men—had to—had to— "By God," he shouted, "let's not wait till any boy comes home crippled in soul, if he isn't in body! Let's tell him what we think of him when he's able to hear and see and feel and know it!"

The mayor was a born leader of men and he swept the town with him. The celebration planned for the first young man to be chosen from Median grew so enormous that every young man who had to register held his head higher because he might be the one. People forgot that in towns all over the nation young men would be chosen the first of the first draft. Everybody felt it was really only the one boy in Median who was to be chosen in Washington on a certain day in October.

Of this the Lims knew nothing because little Siu-lan had met with an accident. Mr. Lim, who had never missed a meeting of the town, now missed the one at which the mayor made his declaration, and this was because of Hen Conolly's boy. One night when he was coming home late from the movies he found a dead cat and, swinging it by the tail, he flung it at someone he saw at the door of the laundry. The heavy inert thing struck full across Siu-lan's narrow little waist. She fell upon the doorstep, and John, carrying her upstairs, saw at once that he must call Dr. Lane.

For a week Mr. Lim went into a silent misery of waiting to see whether there was or was not going to be a grandson. And John did no work He did not leave Siu-lan day or night. Dr. Lane came daily and sometimes oftener, and then Mrs. Lane began to come because the doctor had said to her, "My dear, there seems to be not another woman who ever enters the door down there at Lim's laundry. It isn't a nurse that's wanted—her young husband is handy. But the little creature looks like a Chinese doll and she's so afraid of me she won't let me touch her."

"Why on earth should she be afraid here?" Mrs. Lane exclaimed. She was a kind good woman whom the thought of going to China would have terrified.

"I can't imagine," Dr Lane said, "but see what you can do—the baby's life depends on it."

Mrs. Lane went, though as she stepped over the Lim threshold she felt as nervous as though she were going into an unknown country. "I always was afraid of them, you know—their slant eyes and all," she told her friends.

But when Siu-lan saw Mrs. Lane she knew that here was one American whom she need not fear any more than she would her own mother.

"Has this one any boys?" she asked John at once.

"They are childless, these two," John replied.

Siu-lan smiled at that and put out her small hands, and Mrs. Lane could not keep from taking them, and then it was no time until, as she told Mrs. Penny later, she forgot all about the pretty little thing not being like anybody else.

Together she and Dr. Lane brought Siu-lan back safely to her task of having a grandchild for the Lim family. Mr. Lim would have signed away his whole laundry business in gratitude if the white-haired doctor would have had it. But John said nothing and Dr. Lane noticed it.

"Old Lim is a pleasant kind of fellow—but young Lim is different," he told his wife.

"He doesn't seem to care for a thing unless it's that little girl," Mrs. Lane replied. "He's real nice to her, though."

"Who wouldn't be?" the doctor retorted.

"It wasn't so nice to have a dead cat thrown at you!" Mrs. Lane said.

"That sort of thing ought to be stopped," Dr. Lane agreed. "But what can you do about other people's children?" He rubbed his chin slowly. "Queer how cruel even good enough folks can be without thinking," he said.

"Ain't it!" Mrs. Lane said.

Thus when the mayor announced the day of the drawing of the draft the Lims were not as well prepared for it as were the other citizens of Median. But since all was now well with Siu-lan and she could be left in the care of the two old men, Mr. Lim told John that they must obey the mayor and attend the meeting, and that is why they were both there, not on the front seat where Jim Halley and his father and his mother sat, but just inside the door with the colored janitor.

Never, Mr. Lim thought, had he seen the city hall so beautiful. There were bright papers streamers across the ceiling and vines climbing the pillars and the platform was banked with the best potted plants in Median that in winter were nursed in sunny windows.

Mr. Lim leaned over to his son. "If we had known, we could have brought our potted bamboo."

John nodded, but he said nothing.

The mayor got up to speak. He was very red and spoke loudly.

"It is a pity the mayor excites himself," Mr. Lim whispered to his son. He watched awhile and then leaned over to his son again.

"Is the mayor angry about something?" he asked.

"He seems to be," John said carelessly. What had all this to do with him?

After that Mr. Lim listened closely, and what he heard

was that America was the greatest country in the world, the most independent, the most generous, the richest, the best, and that while all Americans ought to be willing to die for their country and God knows *were* willing, yet it was to be asked why again they had to fight. Mr. Lim wanted to get up and say to the mayor, "Sir, but what if there are nations like Japan?" But he sat still, fearing this would be discourtesy. Nevertheless he rubbed his nose and pulled his ear and after a moment he leaned over to his son again. "Sometimes one *has* to fight," he whispered loudly. But John did not answer. The mayor had paused. The moment had come when at Washington the first number was to be drawn for the first draft of what might be the greatest army in the world. The mayor had planned his speech carefully to this instant. In the silence the atmosphere of the room tightened. People sat up, they leaned forward, heads turned toward the loudspeaker. On the front seat Jim Halley held his head very high, but his mother bent hers and stared at her hands, folded in her lap.

Only John Lim did not move. He sat looking out of the window near him into the cottonwood trees which filled the town square, thinking of himself, his wife, his child to come.

"I have no country," he was thinking.

At this instant the radio came on. The Voice from Washington spoke to Median, as it did to thousands of little towns like it. But not everywhere was there such waiting. On the table was a purse of money which the mayor himself had brought up to five hundred dollars, and there was a silver plaque donated by the merchants of Median to the first American boy to be chosen from their town, and the mayor stood waiting to receive from the radio the number which would tell Median. The mayor's mouth was quivering—though he had nothing but daughters, thank God!

"It takes me back," he said gravely, lifting his voice above the Voice from Washington, "it takes me back to my own young manhood. Of the four of us who went out of Median to that First World War, only I came back. Those other brave boys never knew what their folks thought of them. But today this boy and all our boys will know."

The Voice from Washington said, "The number is one five eight."

Jim Halley heard instantly that it was not his number and he stirred and coughed and pulled up very slightly the creases of his new trousers. He looked at his mother and then at his father. For the moment they felt nothing but disappointment. Since Jim would have to go anyway, sooner or later, it would have been nice if—

Then everybody was looking for a young figure rising to his feet, but none rose.

"Has anyone this number?" the mayor shouted.

There was an echo in John Lim's stunned brain. Slowly he stood up, a slight dark Oriental figure.

"It is I," he said.

The faces of the people of Median turned to him and stared, unbelieving, and he felt the red running to his cheeks as he received into his too sensitive mind what they were thinking.

"I am sorry," he stammered, "it is not my fault." He must find words to go on, to tell them that of course he would not take their—their money, or their honor. He would claim exemption. But before he could speak even the first word, his father rose at his side, his brown old face shining with a light that none had ever seen on it before. Whatever the people of Median were feeling, he did not know it. The radio voice was announcing another number, but nobody heard, for the mayor reached and turned the dial.

"I wish to thank you, sir, Mr. Mayor," Mr. Lim said clearly. "Mr. Mayor, sir, please thank the President in Washington for my family. When I write to my family in Canton that this honor has come to us, that my son has been chosen to be the first to fight for this country where he was born, how shall they express their thanks?"

In speechlessness the people of Median listened.

"Father!" John's voice was a whispered outcry, but Mr. Lim would not hear it.

"Exempting we will not take," Mr. Lim said firmly. "In my country the father also supports son, wife, grandson, as long as needed. I gladly do so here."

John sat down suddenly and gripped his hands. American or Chinese? If he were American he would have the guts now to leap to his feet and speak. "I'll make my own choice, Father—you can't decide this for me!" He could not do it, and his father went on.

"It is now my chance to say how happy I am to have my son to give this country. He is my only son—therefore, most precious. He is the best I have to give. I give him gladly. For I have lived here so many years, and you have let me live here and have given me your business. There has been kindness as well as business. Trouble, too, but we are all humans and trouble is everywhere. The great thing for which I thank you at this time is that you have let me come here looking so different from you, such a skin and eyes, a Chinese. Yes, but my son is American. He is born American. This is the great thing. Whatever the skin and eyes, he can be American. Where else do all colors and kind make their own country? Shall we not fight to save this good country?"

He turned to his son. "John, get up!"

John was a Chinese at the sound of his father's voice.

"I won't go," he was saying wildly in himself, "I won't go!" But aloud he did not speak.

"Thank our friends," his father commanded him. "There is your schoolteacher and his son. Mr. Halley, when I first come here, I speaked no English, but I came to your night class and you taught me. You taught my son at a free public school. We thank you. Sir, in his time the son of such a man as you will do some good things for another like me. We thank you. Mr. Stout, sir, grocer, when business was bad for Depression, three months you let us eat and we could not pay. Could this happen somewhere? No, I think only here. Thanks, Mr. Stout. Recently we had a trouble in our family and Dr. Lane, you, sir, and Mrs. Lane, madam, helped us, how greatly! And Reverend Brown, your church sent money to China for the sick and hungry—thank you—thank you!"

One by one Mr. Lim named half the people of Median and bowed, and what could a Chinese son do but bow with his father? He bowed sullenly enough at first. Then a magic began to work in him as his father brought to life those faces before him. One by one he began to see them—to remember certain things that were not torture.

"Dead cat, hey?" Dr. Lane had said when he told him why Siu-lan had fallen.

The old doctor had looked sheepish.

"And when I was a small boy in another city," he said slowly, "I—I threw an apple core at a Greek. It hit him on the neck and he turned and gave me a look I never forgot. I wonder why I did that. I still feel ashamed."

Warmth stirred uncertainly in John in answer to another warmth he now saw upon these faces as his father recalled their kindness. Yes, there had been kindness. He saw his father sit down at last. But John was still standing. Now he must speak. The people waited kindly for what he would say. His eyes upon these plain friendly faces, he suddenly bowed a small quick bow.

"I agree with my father," he said and sat down.

Everybody clapped and men muttered to each other, "Good old fellow—the Chinese are good folks." As for the mayor, he had, while Mr. Lim was speaking, what afterward he called an old-fashioned conversion. "I suddenly saw what the whole shootin' match was about," he told his wife later. "John Lim," he said, "will you come forward?"

John slid past his father and went up the aisle and stood while the mayor made him the speech he had planned for half a dozen others, at heart secretly for Jim Halley, that handsome fellow. But the mayor was a good man and a just one and he went through the speech exactly as he had memorized it. When John had received the purse and the plaque, had heard himself called the First American of Median, had turned and bowed, the mayor motioned to the band and everybody rose and sang "The Star-Spangled Banner," and John's knees trembled, not with fear of anything except that his heart would grow too big for his bosom and his face break its calm and disgrace not him, but an American. If there were any who felt that it was a pity perhaps—and there were some—these waited until they got home to say so.

Mr. Lim and John walked home in silence. At the door, John stood aside as he always did and let his father go in first. Then he followed. Inside, Mr. Lim took off his hat and coat and tie and put on his apron.

"I will work also if she needs nothing," John said quickly.

"Do not hurry yourself," Mr. Lim said tranquilly, and spat on an iron to test it.

But John was already upstairs. She was in bed, looking so pretty that his heart all but fainted.

"Can you— When I go to war," he began, seizing her little hand.

"Do you go to war?" she gasped.

"I have been chosen," he said.

He showed her the purse, the plaque, the promise of a job if he wanted it, though of course he would come back to the laundry. She listened, her hand clinging to his, her eyes bright with pride in him. Then those eyes clouded.

"Is it safe for me when you are gone?" she asked. "For me and your child?"

He thought a moment and felt an old burden lift itself from his shoulders. What boy, what smallest boy, even, would chalk marks on the door of the first American to be chosen from Median, or would think of calling him "John-John Chinaman"?

"You will be safe here now," he said. "You and our son."

If It Must Be So

"Dr. Steadiman, you simply must!"

James Steadiman looked with kind gravity into pretty little Clare Newman's eyes, blue as a child's.

"I certainly will, if it can be done, Clare," he said.

He remembered her mother, before Clare was born, in this same danger. He hoped Clare had not inherited it, that fatal difficulty in bringing a child to birth. Her mother had lost three children before Clare was born. This was Clare's first. Strange how a woman's body could make a habit for itself! He must somehow keep Clare's slender girl's body from the mischievous trick. She and young Henery Newman so wanted this first baby.

"If you follow my instructions," he said sternly, "I think it can be done. But you must not take the slightest chance."

He could not tell her that it was because of her mother he was now so stern with her—her silly pretty mother who mourned so desperately over her babies born dead and too soon, and yet who could not control her restlessness and stay

in bed. The first time it had been horseback riding—a glorious
September day had done it. And the second time she had
wanted so badly to go to a dance—

"I'll do anything," Clare said earnestly.

"Stay in bed, then, until I tell you to get up," he ordered
her abruptly.

"All right," she answered promptly.

"And I mean in bed!" he said.

"So do I," she replied.

"Then that's all for the present."

He shuffled together the pages of the report the nurse had
given him and fastened them with a clip, and Clare rose,
pulling on her gloves. He smiled at her suddenly. He liked
to see a young woman determined upon motherhood. That
was the way women should be. He might be old-fashioned,
but he believed women should all be mothers, if they were
healthy. Society ought to see to it. Someday he would write
about that, maybe. . . .

"Goodbye, Clare," he said. "Don't worry. We're going to
bring it off."

"I know we are, Dr. Steadiman," she replied. "You'll see—
I shan't slip once."

"Good!" he said heartily. "As for me, I'd rather bring a
fine child into the world than be the President of the United
States."

They laughed and shook hands, and he opened the door
for her into the waiting room. It was long past his noon closing
hour, but he saw there was still another woman there, waiting.
He shut the door and sat down at his desk and looked at
his watch. Half past one—he'd have to telephone Florence
he would be late again for lunch. They'd better go on without
him. He hadn't noticed the time. He'd taken longer than
necessary, perhaps, with Clare, but he was as anxious as she
was. They were a fine young couple, Clare and Henery. He
was doing well, everybody said, in that new television com-
pany. Someday he'd be a rich man. They ought to have a

lot of children. They had everything to give their children—youth, beauty, a good home. . . . He rang the bell sharply. Why didn't Reed bring in the next patient?

The nurse hurried in, apologetic.

"Oh, Doctor, I'm sorry! I just was trying to put her off—it's so late. She hasn't an appointment, but she says she is an old patient of yours. I was coming in to find out what you want to do."

"Who is she?" he inquired.

"A Mrs. Brownley," Miss Reed answered. She glanced at the sheet in her hand. "Charlotte Brownley."

Charlotte Brownley? He had not heard of her in years—not since the local bank failed and Elton Brownley lost his job as cashier. A decent fellow, too—none of it his fault. They'd moved away and he had never heard where they went.

"I'll see her," he said. "And telephone Mrs. Steadiman, please, not to wait for me."

"Yes, Doctor," Miss Reed replied.

She rustled out, starchily, and he sat remembering the Brownleys. They had lived in that white-and-green house on Chestnut Avenue. It had a nice lawn and some flowers. The people who had it now didn't keep it up half as well as it used to look. He'd delivered both of the Brownley children—nice normal births, too, a boy and a girl. They'd been healthy children, nothing but chickenpox and mumps until they were five or six. Then the bank had failed with a lot of others, and they'd moved away somewhere. Strange, he mused, how intimately he came into people's lives and yet, in a sense, not at all. All he could remember now, beyond medical details, was that they paid their bills and were nice, plain people—though, of course, as Florence would have said, not the sort to join the country club. He yawned and suddenly felt tired. He didn't have time for the country club himself, though Florence and his daughter, Phoebe, seemed to think it the center of the universe. . . . Why didn't Reed come back? He rang his bell loudly. The door opened and Miss Reed said a little hostilely, "I'm sorry, Dr. Steadiman. I was just telling Mrs. Brownley—"

"Close the door, will you?" he said curtly. "Of course I'll see Mrs. Brownley."

"Yes, Doctor," she answered faintly, obeying.

But he paid no attention to her.

"Come in, Mrs. Brownley," he said to the patient. He remembered her perfectly now, though certainly, he thought, she must have been ill. He remembered her a well-built, strongly made woman, full of health, and having a gay manner that at the same time held people off somewhat because it made her seem an independent determined sort of woman— the sort who always looked sunburned and a little untidy. Now she was gaunt, her skin was dry and pale, and her dark hair was graying. She was poorly dressed. Something had evidently gone wrong. But she smiled at him with something of her old look.

"Thank you, Dr. Steadiman," she said. She sat down and glanced around her. "It seems nice to be back here. I used to come regularly before Bob and Betty were born. Remember?"

"How are they?" he asked.

"They're—Bob seems all right, but Betty isn't very strong," she said.

She sat, her hands folded in her lap, as if she were very tired. He watched her closely, noting the signs of intense fatigue in her face and bearing.

"And your husband?" he asked.

"He's—pretty well," she answered.

"I don't believe we've met since you moved," he went on. He must ask her why she was here, if she didn't begin herself in the next moment.

"We've moved three times," she said.

She still had her reserved, rather proud air. It was difficult to press her. He remembered once that Florence had said women thought she was stuck-up. She never wanted to join any of their circles and clubs—not that he could blame her for that.

"Dr. Steadiman—" she began, and paused.

"Yes, Mrs. Brownley?" he answered and waited.

She stirred and unclasped her hands, and then clasped them again.

"I've come to ask for advice first," she went on. "You'll perhaps be shocked at what I am going to say. But please don't blame me. I've thought it all out. I know what I have to do."

"It would be pretty hard to shock me," he said, smiling faintly.

But Mrs. Brownley did not return his smile. Instead she fixed her very clear gray eyes on his face and when she spoke it was in her old firm vigorous way.

"Dr. Steadiman, I am pregnant."

"Yes?" he said, and because she paused again, he said to help her, "I'm glad you've come back to me. I remember the other two children very well."

But she seemed not to hear him. She went straight on.

"Dr. Steadiman, I've thought it all out. I can't have this child."

He had honestly said he could not be shocked, but he was. He had plenty of women skirt delicately about the question of avoiding more children, though he never felt he could give out such information casually. When he was younger he had been indignant about it. Only selfish women refused to have children, he had declared. But as he grew older and had more experience, he knew that sometimes women were right. He had conspired for years, for instance, with poor Joan Holtbe, after she found out there was insanity in Philip Holtbe's family. Yes, and she had stuck to it that Philip himself did not know it when he married her. Well, one couldn't be sure. . . . But he'd never had a woman sit in that chair and look him straight in the eyes and say she didn't want her child.

"Well now, Mrs. Brownley," he began, "I'm afraid you've come to the wrong man for that. I simply don't do it, you know."

"I know," she replied, her voice full of quiet bitterness. "You're a respectable physician, and you can't. All I want to know is, where shall I go, Dr. Steadiman?"

He was long accustomed to women in every sort of trouble. He was used to their despair and to their anger and to their tears. But he had never seen a woman look or speak like this, as though she had reached the very foundations of a strong grim patience.

"Will you tell me just how things are with you, Mrs. Brownley?" he asked. "In my experience they are usually better than one thinks."

But she retorted in the same tone of absolute patient sadness, "In your experience they would usually be better, Dr. Steadiman. I know the women you have to take care of—I used to be one of them. We never dreamed of the—the sort of thing I have to call my life now."

He did not speak. He sat looking at her quietly, waiting for her to explain. But she did not explain. Instead she said brusquely, "There's no use in going into everything. I don't want to ask any favors—unless this is a favor. All I ask is, if your own wife didn't want to—if she couldn't bear a child—to whom would you take her?"

He had been waiting for her further confidence. Women always poured themselves out to him. He expected their long half-hysterical complaints when they were in this woman's condition. He had even heard, often enough, their cryings that they wished they weren't having more children, knowing that one day they would murmur self-reproachfully, "How *could* I have? She's the sweetest one of them all! You must just forget what I said, Doctor." Now he felt as though Mrs. Brownley had slammed a door against him.

He said dryly, "In the first place, madam, I cannot imagine such a situation in my own family. In the second place, I cannot possibly recommend to you a physician who would perform an illegal operation. It would be equal to doing it myself." He leaned back to glare a little at Mrs. Brownley.

She leaned forward. "Then," she breathed, "would you do it yourself?"

"No!" he shouted. Now he was really shocked! "No, certainly I would not!"

She looked at him, a small bitter smile tightening her lips. She picked up a pair of brown cotton gloves that had fallen to the floor.

"Then I'll have to shift for myself," she said. "I came to you because I remembered how kind you were—with the children. I don't want to die, particularly now—they're all dependent on me. And I know these operations are—maybe—dangerous. That's all. I'll go now, Dr. Steadiman."

She was actually getting up to go, pulling on her miserable gloves. He saw how badly dressed she was, how inadequately dressed, even, against the chill air of the late November day.

"Sit down," he said irritably. "If I let you go now, it would be like letting you go to suicide. For God's sake—" He swore a little under his breath, and was suddenly aware of being very hungry. "Have you had any lunch?" he demanded.

She shook her head.

He rang the bell and the nurse appeared.

"Get a couple of sandwiches and some coffee sent in, will you?" he ordered her. "Mrs. Brownley's had no lunch, and it's going to take some time before I can get to a diagnosis. And telephone again I won't be home for lunch at all," he added.

"Yes, Doctor," the nurse murmured.

He began cleaning off an end of the desk. "Bet you haven't eaten in a place like this before," he said, trying to be easy with her.

She answered calmly enough, "I've eaten in a good many queer places." And then her eyes softened unexpectedly. "Dr. Steadiman, haven't you heard—anything about us?"

"Not a word," he said, stuffing his stethoscope into a drawer before he sat down. "How could I? All I knew was you moved away and the house was up for sale."

"I never wrote back to anyone," she admitted. "I couldn't."

"Why not?" he asked practically. "It wasn't any fault of your husband's that the bank failed, was it?"

"Oh, no," she said quickly. "That I couldn't have borne. I've been able to bear everything else—until now."

"Always liked your husband," he said.

"Elton's honest as the day," she said. "He's been wonderful—trying to get a job anywhere he could—" She bit her lip. "He's been willing to do anything," she said. Bitterness had come back into her face and voice. "The things he's done—emptied garbage and tended furnaces, and in summer he's caddied on golf links and—and—"

"Good God!" he muttered. "What on earth—"

"There aren't jobs for a man his age," she said fiercely.

"No, but—but why didn't you let us know—" he began.

"We wouldn't!" she cried. Then she said, "Besides, we kept thinking it couldn't last. And he had wonderful letters of recommendation. You don't know it yourself scarcely when things are getting worse and worse with you. You keep thinking it can't be—it can't happen to you—you feel sure it's going to be better next week—or next month—you'll find something, surely. So you don't tell anybody at first because it won't last, and then when it gets worse you can't tell anybody. And you do anything you can—sell everything you own and borrow on all your life insurance—until—until"—she looked at him with eyes full of remembered terror—"you realize it is possible for your children to—to starve."

"Good God!" he whispered.

"And I had a baby then," she said simply.

"Alive?" he asked gently.

She shook her head. "He died before he was a year old—malnutrition, though the doctor said it was bronchitis. He had no resistance. He was always catching something. He'd be three now—Elton Junior. We were crazy about him—but we just can't have any more. If we do, it will mean back to the old starvation."

She pronounced the word with the same accent of terror.

"You mean—you are managing if you don't have this child—?" he began.

"We were on relief," she said quietly. "We went on relief then, before the baby was born. And we've never been able to get off until three months ago, when I found a job in a restaurant. With the few odd jobs my husband gets, we don't quite starve. We've kept the children in school. If I leave this job, we have to go back on relief."

"Was going on relief—unbearable?" he asked, a little diffidently. He meant to go on from that to say that you couldn't advise an illegal act simply because being on relief was repugnant. Many families on relief had children enough, if one were to believe newspaper reports. But he was not prepared for her passionate angry cry.

"Yes, it is—it's intolerable—it's horrible!"

Her face began working so that he coughed and looked away. But nothing could stop her now. She was pouring it out.

"If you'd seen him! You remember my husband, don't you, Dr. Steadiman? He's so *honorable*—why, the bank failure nearly killed him, though he'd had nothing to do with it! When he found they weren't going to pay people anything, I thought he would lose his mind. He kept trying to think of some way they could be paid. He actually went to see Mr. Runcie, the president. He couldn't believe nothing was going to be done."

"Runcie was a scoundrel," he growled. He'd lost money in that himself—not a great deal, he was thankful to say. He'd never trusted the local bank much.

"Yes, he was," she agreed eagerly, "and Elton wouldn't believe it. When he came home and told me—he had to believe it. And we decided to move right away—sell the house and he'd try to get a job. With all his experience, of course we thought he could. But he couldn't. That was the beginning of the Depression, only we didn't know it yet. Banks were closing everywhere."

He nodded, remembering.

She looked at him pitifully, trying to calm herself, trying to smile. "So—you see? That's all. We went down—down—down—moving into cheaper and cheaper places. I mended and patched and kept the children in school. Then when the baby came we hit bottom—and went on relief. And—and I can't bear to go back—because of my husband. It's—it broke him. He was just dazed. You wouldn't have known him."

He did not speak. Still, he thought, she had to know . . .

She lifted her head suddenly. "I have a fair job—first I was a waitress in a restaurant. Last week I was made head waitress. We'd been hoping and praying for it, because what I can earn there, with what he can earn in odd jobs, will just keep us if—if I can stick to it. Dr. Steadiman"—she was leaning toward him, pleading with him—"if you could see the change in him—just the hope of staying free, self-respecting, independent— He's been more like himself than he has been since the bank failed. If you could just see the difference, you'd—you'd know I have to—to do this."

"Does he know?" he asked.

"No," she said. She looked at him with a queer strong defiance. "I don't have to tell him. He's done the best he could—he'd blame himself. Besides, it's I who have the right to decide."

"I'm not so sure," he muttered.

"I am," she replied.

He was so glad to see the door open and the nurse come in with the food that he leaped to his feet.

"Here we are," he exclaimed. "Well, we're ready. Put it here. Now you get along for your own lunch, Reed."

All the time he was thinking that he was at the hardest

decision he'd ever had to make. What did he mean by "decision"? There was only one thing, of course. She had to go on and have the child, relief or no relief. He couldn't honestly—

"Here," he said, "draw up. I'm famished, and I hope you are."

He handed her an unwrapped sandwich and a paper cup of coffee. She made no pretense that she was not famished. She took one mouthful of the coffee and then picked up the sandwich and ate it quickly, though delicately enough. The hand holding the sandwich was strongly made, clean, and rough with work. But he was hungry, too. It made an excuse for not saying anything for a moment.

Then she said suddenly, "You see how it is, Dr. Steadiman."

"Yes, I see that," he answered.

"You can't honestly say I'm wrong, can you?" she asked.

"Not as you comprehend it," he retorted. "The point is, have you comprehended everything? There is often a way out—"

"Do you think I haven't tried—everything?" she demanded. "You don't know what it is to drop lower and lower, nearer and nearer to the brink. You don't do that without having tried—everything. My husband has applied for hundreds of jobs—literally hundreds. It isn't true any more that if you're honest and hardworking you get a job."

He interrupted her. "I can believe that. What I'm thinking about now is—have we the right to deny a new life because an older one would be happier? After all, your husband— how old is he?"

"Fifty-one," she answered. "All right, Dr. Steadiman, I accept that—though his life is worth more to me than any child's could ever be. But grant that a child's is more valuable to society. What about Bob? What about Betty? They've gone to the brink with us. Bob is fairly strong, but Betty is threatened with tuberculosis because of the sort of food she had to have while she was growing up and we were on relief.

She'll never be strong. The first thing I did when I got my job was to buy cream and eggs—for her. She has just begun to gain a little. And Bob is at that age where he can't get enough to eat. And there's the baby—I've lost one child because there wasn't enough to keep it alive, even though we were half starved, trying to do it."

She set the empty plate and cup on the desk. He pushed aside his cup. He wondered, half embarrassed, if he ought to ask her if she'd like the rest of the sandwich he hadn't touched. But he couldn't do it. He could not after all really understand all she'd been through. He kept seeing her as that gay young woman into whose eager arms he had twice put a healthy welcome child. Besides, he had a consultation—he'd forgotten about that. He pulled out his watch. It was a quarter past two—he had only fifteen minutes to get across town.

"I'm afraid I'll have to go," he said hastily.

She rose at once, but he put out his hand.

"Wait—I'm not turning you out. Come back tomorrow—a day won't matter. I must think what I can do."

Her tired set face broke and changed into the old expression again.

"Thank you," she said. "If you could tell me what to do—I'm really terrified—either way. If anything should happen to me, they'd be—lost—just now."

Her mouth quivered and she turned her head a little.

"I can believe that," he said heartily.

The door opened and Miss Reed stood there with his hat and coat.

"Your appointment—" she began.

When he arrived home late in the afternoon he found Florence in their bedroom. She was sitting half-turned sidewise at her toilet table, doing her nails, her gold-colored satin robe falling away from her upright figure to the carpeted floor. The light shone on her smooth reddish hair that was still without a touch of gray, though his own was nearly white and they were the same age. But she looked years younger than forty-nine. She looked much the same, he thought, as she had when he married her twenty-five years ago. Phoebe had been born the next year and Florence had looked badly for a while until they found she needed an operation. Then she picked up again. Of course, there couldn't be any more children. Maybe that was why he felt as he did—because he had desperately wanted more children himself, though he had never let Florence know it. He ought to be glad she had come through it all right.

"I am tired," he admitted. He sat down carefully on her amber satin-striped armchair. "Clare Newman had a kick-up, and I've been there all afternoon."

She said nothing. She never asked about his cases. So he went on.

"She's going to be all right, though I may have to go back. We're dining at home, aren't we?"

She nodded.

"Thank God for that," he remarked. He got up. "I'll go and bathe and change." At the door he paused. "Phoebe in?" he asked.

She did not look up from the long slender hand she was studying.

"Yes," she replied, "for a wonder."

He laughed a little and went on into his own room. Well, he was glad of that, too. Phoebe cheered them all up, bless her. He would not for worlds have acknowledged it, but sometimes at dinner alone with his wife and mother-in-law he felt oppressed, though he did not know exactly by what. They were quite irreproachable in their behavior to him. But women, he thought, lived somewhere in a world of their own, outside of the life-and-death sort of thing that made up his own days. Sometimes he hardly knew what to say to them. And if he didn't talk at the table, little was said. They were both rather silent women, beyond a few remarks on what had happened during the day. It was amazing how like her mother Florence grew. He hadn't noticed it when she was young. She used then to remind him of a tall lily, quiet and aloof in her shyness.

Phoebe, of course, was like him. He could see it even himself, a smiling dark-eyed thing, always surrounded with boys. He didn't pretend to keep up with her beaux. It was all he could do, he declared, to keep up with her current fiancé, though he knew perfectly well, and Phoebe knew he did, that he was joking. She was only having her fling. When the time came, she'd settle down and make a good wife. He thought of Phoebe always with a melting softness under his breastbone. And then he sighed. He had to come to some conclusion about that Brownley woman. All afternoon he had remembered every little while that he had to know by tomorrow what to tell her.

It was at the dinner table that the idea came to him suddenly that he'd ask these three women. His mother-in-law had been telling about some lecture she had gone to in the afternoon. In the interval of half listening to her, which was his habit, his mind had returned to its problem. It was at that moment the idea occurred to him—a good idea, too, for it was essentially a women's problem.

"Look here," he said abruptly when Mrs. Henshaw paused, "I want to ask you three something. Here's a hypothetical case—"

He put the facts of Charlotte Brownley before them tersely, giving no names. It seemed hypothetical enough as he told it, looking across the pleasantly lighted table at the faces of the three women, each with its peculiar good looks and air of cultivation. Around them the room was warm and handsome. A wood fire burned under the white Adam mantelpiece. He was always glad he had been able to provide well for them—given them their setting, so to speak. Poverty had come no nearer to them than the attending of meetings of the Community Chest drive.

He sat back, looking from one face to the other. No one

spoke for a moment while the maid set down the salad plates, and so he had a chance to see them. Mrs. Henshaw's face did not lose its usual expression of white-haired dignity. But he could detect the slight secret embarrassment she always felt when anything relating to sex was discussed in her hearing. As she always said, "When there is so much beautiful and good to think about, why should we—?" He had purposely, for her sake, stressed Mrs. Brownley's poverty rather than her pregnancy. His wife's face seemed unchanged, too, in its rather static good looks. But he knew it so well. There was in Florence's blue eyes, raised to his, a clear practical question. She put it almost at once.

"It seems odd that people on relief can't make up their minds simply—to refrain."

"Florence!" Mrs. Henshaw exclaimed. "Really!"

It was Phoebe who astonished him, Phoebe who a year ago would have rushed into hot demand that something must be done to help the Brownleys so they could have their baby. She said nothing. She bent her head and ate her salad assiduously.

"I do agree with you myself, however, Florence," Mrs. Henshaw went on, "that people could *think* a little more."

"Granted," he said quietly. What was the use of saying—

But Phoebe looked up from her plate and said it for him. "Perhaps they're still in love with each other," she said abruptly.

Mrs. Henshaw stared at her granddaughter with dignity. "I don't see what that has to do with being able to support another child," she remarked.

"Oh, don't you?" Phoebe exclaimed.

"Phoebe, be quiet," her mother commanded. "As your father says, it's a practical problem. I suppose it's a real one, James?"

He nodded. "Only too real."

"Yes, I thought so," she said capably. "Well, if you really want my opinion, as a practical problem it's this—no reputable doctor would perform an illegal operation, and he couldn't send her to another sort."

"I don't see how," Mrs. Henshaw retorted. "She's perfectly able to have the child, isn't she?"

He could not deny this and she took his silence for assent.

"As to ethical," Florence went on in her positive clear fashion, "it's not even an illegitimate child. There are always ethical grounds against that—"

"If we must discuss this," Mrs. Henshaw said in quiet distaste, "it seems to me the point is that she simply deserves what she got. If we're going to begin letting people—do things—to escape the consequences of something they chose to do in the first place, then all law and proper moral instinct is gone. Where would we be?"

She threw the question out. For a moment he thought Phoebe would answer it. She lifted her head and her dark eyes blazed at her grandmother. But Mrs. Henshaw was now helping herself to roast chicken and did not see her, and Phoebe looked down again. He waited a moment.

Then he said, "Phoebe?"

Her eyes turned, startled, to him. The blaze was gone.

"Yes, Father?"

"What do you think?"

"I? I don't know. I suppose—everybody—has to decide for himself."

He was surprised at her hesitation—it was not like Phoebe to be unsure of herself.

"There is a higher law," Mrs. Henshaw began with unwonted energy. He looked up and met his wife's annoyed look. She lifted her eyebrows. "There," her eyes said, "now you've started her!" He interrupted Mrs. Henshaw. It would not do to let her get angry with Phoebe.

"You've all been helpful except Phoebe," he said, smiling, and trying to make his voice playful. "And Phoebe is being her usual contrary self, Mother, so don't pay any attention to her."

After dinner he would make it up to Phoebe by a little special coaxing. She understood you couldn't upset an old lady with a high blood pressure.

"I see, by the way," Florence said in her equable pleasant manner, "that steel went up today."

"Oh, things are on the up again," he said heartily.

Mrs. Henshaw, always diverted by the movement of stocks, forgot everything else. "I hope that means I get some dividends," she remarked. "I'm getting a little tired of not having any."

He met his wife's eyes and she nodded ever so little and smiled. It was all right—only he mustn't forget to make it up to Phoebe. Three generations of women—sometimes, he grumbled privately to himself, Eliza on the ice had nothing on him!

But there had been no chance to make it up to her. Immediately after dinner a young man came in, someone he didn't know, though Phoebe had cried out he did. There was a vaguely hurt look in the young man's face when the doctor put out his hand and murmured, "I don't believe I know—" And Phoebe had said impatiently, "Oh, nonsense, Dad—it's Fenn Whiteside."

Well, they all looked alike. . . . He sat around awhile after she was gone, and then he knew he'd better go into his study and work on an article he was doing for a medical journal. And he had to think, too, about this confounded Brownley business.

He left his wife and her mother playing cards and went into his study and took up his manuscript and began writing slowly from his notes. All the time he was thinking that he could not possibly perform the operation. In the first place, what about his own risk? Ethical—it was the only possible grounds one could put it on. But what court would recognize it? Suppose it were found out? Or suppose it were not? The law was the law. And in the medical profession above all others, one had to be a stickler, or else one fell too easily into the hands of the doctors who had a shadow on their records. There couldn't be a shadow of a shadow, even, on a doctor. And there would be, even if no one knew but himself—and her. Besides, he didn't know her. He'd be entrusting his whole medical reputation to a woman. A law might be wrong, but as long as it was there— He sighed, and wrote steadily on for a long time, the other thing simmering in the back of his brain.

He had not the least idea of the time when his wife came in to say good night.

"Still working?" she asked. "Hasn't the day been long enough, dear? It's nearly midnight."

"I'd better finish," he replied. No use going to bed with this thing buzzing in his mind like a bee against a window-pane.

She bent and kissed him, and he smelled the fresh fragrance of her scent. He smiled at her. She made him a good wife— left him alone. It was a great thing for a man whose day was filled with women. He could come home to rest. He clung to her hand a moment.

"You do feel I can't do anything about that case?" he asked a little pleadingly.

"Oh, definitely not," she replied. "Besides," she added, "it would be quite dangerous professionally, wouldn't it?"

"I suppose so," he admitted.

"And that sort of thing always leaks out," she said. "You can never be sure people won't tell. And the public never believes in good motives."

"No," he agreed.

"Don't sit up all hours," she begged him, drawing away her hand and touching his cheek delicately before she was gone.

It was all very well, he thought, sitting there alone, but women were so strangely cold to women. They always blamed a woman. Old Mrs. Henshaw distinctly felt the woman ought to suffer it.

The door opened a crack and then wider, and Phoebe looked in.

"Hello," she said.

"What's the matter with you?" he asked. "I thought dawn was the end of your day."

"Oh, I was bored," she said. "I left the crowd."

She came in and sat down on the chair opposite him. She was a pretty thing, he thought. But then he always thought that whenever he had a chance to look at her. Not that it ever went further than a moment's look at her! She was busy all the time. Whenever he thought of her he saw her mentally poised for a hasty kiss, on her way to lunch or tennis, riding or dancing. Someday they'd have to talk about her settling down, only not when she was so pretty. This part of a girl's life was as ephemeral as a butterfly's in May.

"You don't get bored easily, I hope?"

She shook her head at him brightly. "No, only sometimes. Tonight it seemed to me suddenly that I'd been a million times to the Glass Slipper."

"That where they were going?"

She nodded without speaking, and he sat watching her.

"That woman," she said suddenly, not looking up at him. "I haven't been able to forget her."

"Nor I," he answered.

"Your case?" she asked. Why did she sound a little breathless?

"Used to be," he answered.

"What are you going to do?" she asked, still not looking up.

"Darned if I know," he said. "Probably end up telling her I can't do anything. I don't see that I can take the responsibility."

"You're taking much more that way," she said sharply.

"What do you mean?" he asked. He'd never seen Phoebe's pretty round face look like this. She looked suddenly older, saddened. He saw her ten years from now, hit by something—

"If you send her away, she might be desperately ill—die, maybe."

He did not answer. Good God, how did she know about such things?

"They're filthy," she said in a low voice.

"Who?" he asked, amazed.

"The sort of doctor she'd have to go to," she replied.

He had heard one way and another about the way girls were nowadays. It had never occurred to him that what he heard had anything to do with Phoebe. She might be a flirt, but then what pretty girl wasn't? It was natural—healthy instinct working and yet defending itself, too. But then of course girls talked. But she looked up at him suddenly and he saw a queer anger in her eyes.

"I can't understand any of it," she said passionately. "Everything encourages you to go ahead—society urges people to—to marry and all that. Then it clamps down on you. A girl—a woman gets into an impossible position—and even a decent doctor won't tell her what to do!"

"But what can I tell her?" he inquired, astonished. "How can I help the law?"

"If you don't do something for her, Dad," she said irrelevantly, "I'll never respect you as much again."

"No, but, Phoebe—" he began. What was this nonsense? He oughtn't to have said anything. What the deuce had prompted him to break his rule and say anything about a patient?

"Your grandmother and mother don't agree with you," he ended rather feebly.

"They don't know anything about it," she said.

"But, Phoebe—" he began.

"Neither do you," she interrupted.

He felt out of patience with her. "I shall have to do what I think best," he said with dignity.

"Then you won't do anything," she said angrily.

"Not necessarily," he insisted.

"Yes—necessarily!" she cried. She was so unlike herself that he did not know what to say next.

"Mind you, it's a test," she went on excitedly. "It's a test of your generation! Here you are, up against a real situation—on one side the law, on the other a human being. Which is the more important to you?"

He did not answer. He sat looking at her steadily.

"There's something queer about you," he said.

Looking at her, he might have been seeing a patient—eyes dilated, hands trembling a little, a decidedly hysterical note in the voice.

"What's up, my dear?" he asked. "It's not this woman. You don't know her. Come, tell me!"

To his horror, she answered by covering her face with her hands and breaking into crying. Phoebe, on whom he depended for gaiety in his house!

"Why, darling!" he whispered. He rose and went over to her and tried to put his arm around her. But she sat, an obdurate unyielding young creature.

"Oh, it's too late for it to be any good to *me*," she sobbed. "I don't see why I care now, one way or the other, what you do. I'd rather you *didn't* help her, in one way. Then I'd know I was right—about all of you."

"All of us?" he repeated, mystified.

"You and Mother and Grandmother," she said behind her hands, "you're all alike. What do you know—about anybody? Only for a moment, at dinner, I wondered if I'd been wrong about you."

Right about them—wrong about him—what was she talking about?

"Suppose you just say what you mean," he said. He sat down again.

"Will you help her if I tell you?" Phoebe suddenly lifted her eyes to him.

He thought a moment. "I'll do something," he promised. "I won't just send her away."

She looked at him with strange suffering eyes. "No, Dad—because—it's fearfully dangerous—the other thing. I know—*because I did it!*"

He stared at her, not for a second understanding. Then he understood, and the blood ebbed out of his heart. The room sprang out at him, her tense face, her shining dress and hair, her hands fallen in her lap—Phoebe sitting there. Not another woman—not a patient—little Phoebe—

"You didn't tell me," he said in a thick voice.

"I was afraid to," she said simply.

Who was the fellow? His brain flung out questions. When had it happened? How could it possibly have escaped his notice?

"You don't mean to say—under my eyes—" he muttered.

"No. It was my last year—at school. I didn't come home Easter vacation, remember?"

"But you were a child!" he cried, and his voice wailed in his own ears.

"Not really," she said, a little sadly.

No, he wouldn't ask anything! Two years ago! Two years she had had this horrible thing in her memory!

"You might have died," he said, choking.

"I nearly did," she said.

"I'd have thought of something," he said. "You ought to have told me. I'd have done it—myself—"

It wouldn't have been a child, he thought frantically. It would have been like cutting out any other unwanted growth.

"Would you have broken the law for me?" she was asking him.

"Damn the law!" he cried.

Her lips quivered. "I don't think I ever dreamed then that you would," she said. "I thought of you simply as a respectable doctor. It didn't occur to me—"

He did not answer. He sat yearning over her, his mind flying through unspeakable detail.

"That doctor—" he said abruptly.

"Don't!" she whispered. "I can't tell you anything. Don't ask me. Only if I can save any woman from it, I must. Tell her—tell her—if you won't do it—to go back on relief—to—to—"

Her eyes were sick, and he groaned.

"Oh my God, Phoebe!" He felt actually nauseated.

She looked away from him for a moment. Then she leaped to her feet and rushed into his arms. He could feel her shaking with weeping and suddenly he began to weep, too.

"Oh, Phoebe girl," he muttered.

"It's no good crying," she was sobbing into his neck. "It's all over. I'm—all right—if I don't think. But it was so awful—not being able to come to you."

He held her, stricken and cursing himself. His own daughter—and she could not come to him!

She gave him a convulsive squeeze. "Don't worry about me," she whispered. "I'm—over it."

She was gone. He heard her flying up the stairs. His arms felt empty. He sat down again, dazed, trying to remember just what it was she had said—how, indeed, she had come to say it at all. He felt guiltily that he did not even know whether or not he was glad she had told him. For what would he do with this awful knowledge?

He dragged himself upstairs to bed at last. At the door he paused, listening. He could hear nothing. He opened the door slowly, without noise. The light from the hall shone across her face. She was asleep. He closed the door again. How could she sleep like that? He marveled until he remembered that, doubtless, there had been nights enough when she had not. He went to his own room in an ague of misery.

He rose the next morning in a heavy fatigue, not having slept all night. His wife detected it at once. She looked at him across the breakfast table.

"You seem nervous this morning, James," she remarked.

"Didn't sleep," he muttered.

"I'm afraid you worried about that woman," she went on.

He did not deny it. "Clare Newman must be all right," he said instead. "I didn't get a call."

What he was really nervous over was the danger of Phoebe's appearing. He didn't want to see her—not until he knew what he was going to do.

But he needn't have worried. She didn't show up. He rushed through and hurried away. Then when he put his hand into his right glove, he found a little note there, folded into a neat square. He opened it and saw Phoebe's handwriting.

"Darling Dad—I've slept like a babe. Why didn't I have the sense before to come to you?"

That was all. No begging, no mention of last night or of Charlotte Brownley—just how she felt toward him.

He thought, "It's six of one and half a dozen of the other. There's the law to risk on one hand, and on the other Phoebe!" He winced, thinking of how Phoebe had stood in such horrible need and he hadn't seemed a man she could talk to, let alone a father. That was what broke his heart—that his profession made women come to him, but not his own daughter in a woman's need. The Law versus Women—there was the case for him. He had to be judge, plaintiff, defendant, and jury, all together.

He entered his own waiting room. It was already full of women. He plowed through them in his usual fashion without looking at them. On his desk was his schedule. The nurse was waiting.

"Mrs. Newman called to say she'd had a good night."

"Fine," he said, reading down the list of closely packed hours. It would be a nice mess if he were arrested for an illegal operation—all his years of carefully built reputation gone in a whiff of slander! He could use ethics of therapeutics for an excuse—no, he'd have to say simply that he did what he thought was right—if he thought it *was* right, of course.

That was the question. As for Reed, he'd simply tell her it was therapeutics. She'd been with him for years—besides, she had a rabbit brain and he was her god. In a pinch, she'd swear to anything he told her.

He drew a line through the last appointment.

"See if you can change that," he ordered the nurse. "I may want that hour free for an operation."

He knew that he could have done nothing else the moment he saw Mrs. Brownley's face when he went into the operating room. He carried the shadow already, of course. He would carry it as long as he lived. But he'd have to carry the shadow of Phoebe anyway. There was no escape from what existed. The law didn't prevent anything—he saw that now. It just made a breeding place for quacks. No, that wasn't the point for him. Generalizations weren't his business. This woman—and his Phoebe—they were his facts—he had to face them and he would.

Charlotte Brownley said, "You can trust me."

But he did not even answer. He was suddenly too proud to ask for secrecy. He simply said, "Thanks—but I am doing what I think is right." He paused, and went on firmly, "It's what I'd do for my own daughter—if she were in the same position."

With those words it was all clarified and became inevitable. He went on doing his good clean sterile job. . . .

He went into his wife's room before dinner.

"Phoebe home?" he asked.

"In her room, I think," she answered.

"I want to see her a minute," he said.

He knocked on Phoebe's door and heard her light voice. "Who is it?"

"Me," he said, going in.

She stood, wrapped in a rose-red dressing gown, brushing her flying dark hair before the mirror. At his entrance she turned, half startled, and paused.

"Dad!" she cried.

He nodded. "You won," he said.

"Oh!" she whispered. She looked at him, her face lighting into joy. Then she flung herself upon him. He knew, his cheek on his child's soft hair, that he had chosen the lesser shadow. He could never have borne anything other than this look in her face, this—adoration.

She lifted her head to ask him, "Is she all right?"

"Perfectly—if I do say it."

She looked at him with wet eyes. "Why didn't I know what you are?"

He shook his head. "Don't. I don't know now if I've done the right thing—though I told her I did."

"I say you did!" she cried.

He did not answer. He was suddenly desperately tired. She was probably right—the young usually were right, at least for tomorrow. After all, he'd been trained yesterday—when the law was made.

"Going out?" No use talking about what was done, so long as they were close like this.

"Yes, I was. Would you rather I didn't?" She drew back to look at him.

"Of course not. I want you to have a good time."

She floated away from him happily. "Oh, I'm going to have a wonderful time!"

He watched her. . . . After it was over, Charlotte Brownley had wept suddenly.

"What are you crying for?" he had asked.

"I don't know," she had sobbed. Then she had wiped her eyes resolutely and said, "Yes, I do—sheer gratitude."

"Sure that's all?" he had demanded. "Because it's too late for anything else."

"Sure!" she had answered. . . .

"I feel so—eased!" Phoebe whispered. She flew at him again. "I love you, Dad!"

He stood, thinking, under her embrace.

"I won't say anything now," he thought—only he must have a look at her. God knew what that quack might have done to her. He suffered a stab of agony again. Think of a wretch like that hacking at his Phoebe's lovely body! . . . The Brownley woman had come in today absolutely determined. She was going straight on to a quack. . . . He had saved her, anyway.

"Oh, I'm going to dance and dance, I'm so happy!" Phoebe was saying.

"That's right," he said.

He went to the door. Well, it was all over. He wasn't sure a lot of wrongs totaled up to a right. The only thing that was an absolute right was the good clean job he'd made of it. Queer comfort, maybe—especially when he knew he'd wake up often enough wondering what he would do if— But a good clean job was always right. That and Phoebe dancing and happy were the two absolutely right things in the world. He'd stick to them.

The Castle

From where Julian sat upon a flat rock, he could see the landscape of three counties of England. He knew every dip and hollow of the green hills, for it was the same view which could be seen through the end window of the long gallery. Here in Monteith Castle he had been born and here he had lived all his life until the war, except for school. The gray stone wall behind his back was warm with the sun of this mild spring day, and the earth under him was warm, too, and only slightly damp. He sighed and closed his eyes and his mind shed the problem of his life. So had he been used to do in the years when he was a little boy, which now seemed so long ago. This curve in the stone wall of the castle had hidden him from nurses and tutors and parents, and here he had made his dreams.

Castle and lands were his now, although in this present England one ought perhaps to be ashamed of owning a castle. Still, it was scarcely his fault. Centuries of ancestors had lived here before him and each owner had handed the castle on to his son, repaired and changed enough to bear the sign of his own time upon it. Kings had slept here as guests, and as ungrateful guests they had sometimes seized the castle as a home for a mistress or a friend. But the Monteiths were stout folk, and somehow or other a Monteith had always got Monteith Castle back again.

At the end of so long a family tree, he should, he sometimes thought, be a weakling, a degenerate of one kind or another, but he thought of himself as an ordinary chap. That is, he was a tall strong ruddy-faced young man who looked well in a uniform. He had the big Monteith nose but not as big as his grandfather's had been.

He kept his eyes closed, but he was not asleep. His grandfather would have been properly horrified if he could have seen what was going on inside Julian's skull just now. It would not have occurred to old Julian that any descendant of his could think that Monteith Castle was anything but a joy to possess. But old Julian could not in madness have imagined this England. Young Julian opened his eyes and set his lips. He sat up and hooked his big thin hands loosely over his knees. The damp was beginning to creep through the gray tweed of his suit. He got up and, still leaning against the wall, he stared thoughtfully over the landscape. If anyone had told him that he could consider giving up Monteith Castle, he would have felt like knocking his block off. Monteith Castle owned him really, as it had owned his forefathers. He would die as they had, but the Castle would go on forever. Even if it were used as a museum or a jail or whatever the lot of them might want it for, it would still be Monteith Castle, its walls belonging to history. How many Monteiths had gazed as he did now, over the Three Counties! The landscape this spring morning was as peaceful as one of the Corots in the long gallery. Softly green, vaguely spotted with pink of newly opening apple trees, nothing moved. Even the cows stood still in the valley as they fed upon the tender grass, and upon a distant hill the sheep were no more than a white mist.

Suddenly his roving eye caught a small moving figure. Along

the old highway at the foot of the hill a girl on a bicycle came to a stop. She was too far away for him to see more than her slight, rather tall figure, in a gray-blue suit, but he could see her blond hair shining in the sunlight. She seemed in two minds whether to stop or go on. For a moment she stood still, gazing toward the castle. Then suddenly she laid her cycle carefully on the turf and began to climb the hill in long lithe strides. He shrank back against the wall, making himself as much as possible a part of its grayness. He didn't want to have to talk to a sightseer—and a girl.

It was no use. He could not hide himself. Her gaze picked him out inexorably and she approached him, one hand in her pocket, the other clasping a pair of old leather gloves. As she came near he stared into a pair of very clear blue eyes, but he made no move toward pleasantry.

"I beg your pardon!" Her crisp voice actually begged nothing.

Ah well, at least it was English—not American or French or any of the other voices he had heard too much of in recent years! He allowed himself a cool response. "Good morning."

"Will you tell me if this is Monteith Castle?"

"It is."

She received this news with only mild interest. "I didn't come to see it—I'm on my way to Lyddington."

"Really?"

"Yes."

She paid no further attention to him as she surveyed the high gray walls, the two huge towers of the gate, and the dry moat, which on the map hanging in the great hall was marked "The Mighty Dytche."

"William the Conqueror, I suppose?" she asked.

"So they say," he replied.

Her skin was smooth and pale, and her small mouth was barely touched with pink. He was glad to see that she wore no nail polish and that her clothes looked decently old and well cared for. He had begun to feel more kindly toward her, perhaps even to the point of a remark, when she said, "I have one, too—perhaps a bit bigger."

"What?" he asked. He hoped she was not one of those hop-skip-jump people who talked ahead of his thoughts.

"A castle," she replied.

He shrugged his shoulders. "Then you know what it's like. This one's mine."

"Really?" Her blue eyes opened at him.

He nodded.

"You can't live in it!" she exclaimed.

"Why not?" he retorted. "I do."

"But how can you?" she inquired. "We have to live in our gatehouse. Poor Father!"

"Depends on what you call living," he said. "The staff is skeleton."

"Of course," she said carelessly.

She seemed to forget him then, for she sauntered slowly away, looking at the walls and at the green landscape. Since she had disturbed his peace, he allowed her to go. Then he followed her—why, he did not know. The air was so warm, the sun so unusually clear that it was impossible to ask for reasons, even if he had been interested in reasons, which he never was. The castle, which could be a place of gloomy medievalism on a rainy day, was beautiful under the blue sky. The knots of green ivy upon its walls were decorations.

He found her standing at the gate between the towers. "You may go in if you like," he told her. "There hasn't been a portcullis in five hundred years. I believe Edward the First repaired the towers."

"You're a bit older than I am," she said. "I only go back six hundred years."

"I'm nine hundred," he murmured.

The shadows between the towers were sharp, almost as sharp as he had seen shadows in Egypt. One didn't often get sun like this in England. "If you're in the gatehouse," he said, "who's in the castle?"

"My brother's the heir," she answered. "He's there, to save death taxes."

"I have no heir, unfortunately," he said.

"Aren't you married?" she asked entirely without coquetry.

"No," he said.

"Naturally, if you want an heir . . ." She left the sentence hanging as being too obvious to finish.

"Quite," he agreed.

But she was uninterested and, apparently forgetting what they were talking about, she exclaimed at the sight of his old sheepdog that lay in the sun of the courtyard like a thick gray mat. She hastened between the towers and knelt beside the beast and rubbed its ears. "What an old darling!" she murmured. Then when the dog did not move she asked, "Is he ill?"

"He doesn't notice anyone except me," he replied. "He belonged to my father originally. Of course he oughtn't to be alive, but—"

"I'm glad you keep him," the girl said with a soft intense tenderness. "One shouldn't kill things just because they are old."

She stood up and he, divining that she was about to go, thought of how to detain her. Her face now was quite lovely, feeling and moved as she looked down at the dog. The slight unconscious haughtiness he had seen about her before was gone.

He asked, "Would you like a personally conducted tour or have you enough of castles?"

She hesitated. "There's something about them—"

He hastened to hold this small interest, perhaps only a courtesy.

"Well then, there's where the old keep was—you'll see it's been made into a garden. That was done three hundred years ago by another Julian for his wife. My grandfather was a Julian, too, and his bit was to put up the gallery. Shall we go inside?"

She hesitated again. "Let's not," she said. "Do you mind?

The sun's so wonderful. I daresay it never gets inside. It never does in ours. The windows are slits."

"It's fair in the gallery," he said. "The windows are modernish."

"Well, only the gallery, then."

"You'll have to go through the great hall at that."

"Only the great hall, then."

But when they were in the great hall she pointed at the tall chest. "That's nice!"

He smiled. "King James left it when he last visited and it's still here, waiting."

She laughed. "Forgetful, wasn't he?"

"A good many bits were forgotten," he replied. He led the way across the stone floor, which when he was a little boy had kept his knees always skinned. "Walk on the rugs— do, Master Julian!" his nurse had cried, but he'd had a game of his own which compelled him to skip the rugs. He skipped them now by habit unless he made himself remember how odd it looked when one was six feet four inches tall. He remembered and he led the way decorously toward the gallery.

"The Virgin Queen," he announced, flinging his hand toward a ruffled portrait. "Surrounded by my relatives, I'm afraid. They were frightful snobs."

"So were mine," she replied. "Still are, for that matter. I suppose yours moan a lot about Government?"

"They're kicking in their graves, I daresay," he said.

"You mean you're the only living Monteith?"

"Except for some old distaff cousins somewhere in Cornwall," he replied.

She looked thoughtful at this. Then she said quietly, just as they were entering the long gallery, "It must upset you frightfully, thinking what to do with this all alone."

"It does," he said. "Duty, and all that—"

They stood looking up the endless room. The walls were hung with paintings, and the silver-green carpet, woven of silk, was deep as moss beneath their feet. Satin-covered chairs and sofas stood beside inlaid tables. When he was small he had cleared a passageway between them and he had run races with the dog. That was on rainy days. Other days he had spent from dawn to dark upon the hills.

"Let's go outside again," she said suddenly. "But it's a handsome gallery. I congratulate your old Julian. And you're Julian, too."

He nodded and led her to a tall door that opened upon a terrace which his own father had put in because, he complained, it tired him to walk the length of the gallery to get to the south lawn.

"Cigarette?" he asked when they were outdoors.

"Thanks," she replied. She sat down on the stone while he searched for his lighter. When he lit the cigarette he noticed that her lashes were long and golden brown. She smoked, her face turned toward the landscape. For so young a creature, she was strangely serene, almost patient. He sat down near her, but not too near.

"I'm so glad I'm a woman," she said at last. Her eyes were still on the landscape and he could look at her face. She was not quite pretty, after all—a trifle too pale. But her features were delicate, and with any effort—or perhaps even a little more good food—she could be very pretty. Whether she would ever make the effort was doubtful, even when food might be plentiful again. Her mind seemed on other things.

"Why?" he asked.

She turned her face to the great gray pile of the castle. "What to do with castles! I shouldn't like to have to decide that. My brother has two sons, and I suppose he feels things will last his lifetime and perhaps theirs—I don't know. But it's not like being able to look hundreds of years ahead as well as behind—the way our ancestors did."

"What is your castle, by the way?" he asked.

"Guilford, in Sussex," she replied simply.

"I say," he exclaimed, "I believe I know your brother. He wouldn't know me, though."

"He was at Oxford."

"So was I—miles behind him, of course. Isn't he a tall dark chap?"

She nodded. "The only black one among us. A Spanish mistake somewhere, my father always says."

"And if you were in his place you wouldn't do as he's doing?"

"I don't know. That's why I'm glad I'm a woman—I don't have to know."

She rose, suddenly in haste, and he found himself shaking a narrow hand. "Goodbye. It's been nice of you to let me see things. If you're ever over our way, look in. My parents would be glad and so would Rodney—that's my brother."

"You haven't told me your name. Think of me not asking it straight away!"

"Mary," she said.

"Lady Mary of Guilford," he repeated.

"Yes," she said quietly.

To his surprise, he was reluctant to let her go. She gave him a smile, and while he stood looking after her she walked with smooth swiftness down the road. Leaning on the wall of the terrace, he saw her disappear behind the oak grove and watched her mount her cycle and ride away until she became a small moving dot upon the road. Then she was lost behind a hill.

He continued to stand, staring at the landscape. The encounter had been so brief, so casual, that surely it was meaningless. Yet it had moved something in him which he had all but forgotten. He was an only child, and he could scarcely remember his mother. She had died the first year when, ridiculously young and much against her will, he had been sent away to school. But he had loved his strong young father, and his father had declared that he must go to school or he would grow up soft. So he had wanted to go to school. Only now did he remember how his mother had clung to him when they parted. He had been uncomfortable, his face buried in the softness of her shoulder, but he had yielded to her, since he would not see her again for a long time. He had been desperately homesick for her at school, at least for the first week, but he had not told her so.

Now, strangely, he wished he had told her. She had died before the Christmas holidays, so he had never seen her again. She had died in her sleep one night. There had been no illness, no time for special letters—nothing. His aunt had come to take her place, his father's older sister, a gaunt-faced kindly woman who saw to it that he was fed and clothed and that the affairs of the castle went on as usual. His mother's rooms were closed, and no one spoke of her to him.

His father never married again. "You'll give me heirs, Julian," he told his son, years later, "and that's all I want out of life now. I shouldn't like to see anybody else than a Monteith in this old place."

"Why?" Julian asked.

"We've always been here," his father said vaguely.

Gazing across the noon-bright landscape, he remembered now things he had long forgotten—how his mother looked as she walked down the long gallery, and how she used to sit upon a cushion on this stone balustrade and watch the summer landscape. She did not look like the girl who had cycled away from him a few minutes ago. She was small and dark-haired and almost excitably gay, unless she carried herself in the same way, head high and eyes straight ahead. There was the same look of dream about them.

The door of the gallery opened and he heard a mild footfall behind him. "Yes, Bram?" he said without turning.

"The fish is just nice now, sir." Bram's thin high voice replied.

"Very well, I'll be in."

"Yes, sir."

He waited until he heard Bram's footsteps retreat and then he went by the outside path to the other side of the house and up another terrace to French doors which were open to the sunshine. Inside these doors a small table had been set for him. The sunshine made a little room for him of light, beyond which the vast dining room lay in shadow. It had been built in Tudor times by an ancestor who, disliking the banqueting hall as a place to dine, had made that into the great entrance hall. Each generation had left its mark upon the castle. Now it was finished. Taxes and upkeep strangled the income of the land, and there could be no more building.

He was not sorry. His father had put in bathrooms and fairly modern kitchens and there was electricity in the new rooms, although the old oil lamps hung in the rest of the castle. Even had he been sure of living here the rest of his life, he would not have added or taken away—unless, perhaps, he could plant some more trees. He had a feeling for trees, and the beeches and oaks were very old. But it was no good planting trees unless one could look ahead for hundreds of years.

He went into a small lavatory off the dining room which his father had put in to use when he came from the farms, and then he sat down to his solitary meal. The food was what it usually was: a soup whose origin he could not guess, fried fish and potato cake, a green he disliked but ate from habit, and then a cheese savory. Bram served as though it were all that it was not, and at least there was a good white wine. His father had laid down enough wine to last two generations of moderate drinkers and Julian declared sometimes that he would keep the castle for the wine, at least.

Actually, he was conscientious and sensitive and the real problem of his life was whether anyone ought to have castles nowadays and, if not, whether he should give his castle to Government for a rest home or a sanatorium or a museum or whatever they saw fit to make it, and take his place among the common folk who had never lived in castles. He sat in the House of Lords as his father had sat before him and he listened with bent head when an old lord got up and railed against the men in office. He never applauded, for, though he sympathized with the old warrior, yet he sympathized, too, with the earnest men who had risen from labor in mines and factories. There was John Pound, whom he had met accidentally one day on the street—they had collided so forcibly that the man had staggered against an iron lamppost. Of course Julian had stopped to see that the hurt was not severe, and then they had walked along together. John Pound, in his first year in the House of Commons, was lit with energy and optimism and enthusiasm.

"You like this Government?" Julian had asked.

"Could I not!" John Pound had retorted. He was a short dark vivid young man. "Look, my father was always on the dole. I never remember his having a job."

"What was he?" Julian had asked.

"An engineer—wanting to build. He sat about doing nothing. What that can mean in a house!" A tragic shadow passed over John Pound's square face. "Well, it won't happen again," he said firmly.

Julian had lunched now and then with John Pound and had listened to him talk. Pound loved to talk. He bubbled over with plans, with admiration for his superiors, and with certainty of the brightness of England's future. Not once had Julian dared to let him know about the castle.

After a month or so of the accidental friendship, he had gone one day to lunch in his usual spot and had found John waiting for him with so pretty a young woman that Julian most unwillingly acknowledged her to be the prettiest girl he had ever seen.

"This is my sister Betty," John said. She was small and very dark, her eyes and hair black, and her skin a warm cream. But they weren't common eyes and hair. Her eyes were large, her hair was softly curly, and she had a sweet small voice and a small firm hand that soon learned as the weeks went on to fit itself into Julian's hand. The first time he felt those fingers in his palm he trembled and thrust them away. He was afraid of women. His father had made him value highly his own body.

"A gift, my son," his father had said. "Generations of Monteiths went into the making of you. Your body is about as perfect as such making can do. You're lucky. Sometimes the process becomes too fine and goes to seed, like an overbred plant. But you're the flower. Don't waste yourself around the countryside. Be grateful and marry young!"

Betty laughed when he pushed her away. She held out her small hands. "They're clean," she declared, her eyes roguish. "I washed them before I came."

"Don't be silly," he retorted feebly. But he did not reach for her hand.

After they had known each other a month he told her about the castle. It seemed only fair. She listened thoughtfully and for once he saw her face when it was utterly serious.

"Don't tell John," he warned her.

"Why not?" she asked.

He felt himself blush. It would sound too absurd to suggest that the castle might make a difference between John Pound and himself.

"John wouldn't care," Betty said gently. "And I tell him everything."

"Do you think it's wrong to have a castle?" he blurted.

She continued her grave and thoughtful look. They were walking along the street, side by side, and she thrust her hands into the pockets of her tweed jacket. "I shouldn't like to have to live in one," she said at last.

Whatever it was that had been about to blossom between them stayed itself at her words. They walked in silence to the next turn and there she stopped and faced him. "Thanks awfully for telling me," she said in her soft voice.

"You don't like me as well," he said abruptly. His hands, too, were deep in the pockets of his topcoat. Thus they faced each other.

"I do like you," she insisted. "Only it takes a bit of thinking."

"I am just the same," he urged.

She considered this while the cool spring wind blew small

curls about her face. "You can't be blamed for being born in a castle," she said at last with some decision. "It all depends on what you do with it from now on."

She gave him a little nod, her dark eyes very bright, and without taking her hands from her pockets she left him, walking with her shoulders straight and square and not looking back.

He liked her more than ever he had. After that he wondered if he could love her—if she let him. When the weekend came he left London and went home for a few days alone to find out. Whatever his decision was to be, it would not be fair to make it away from here.

Bram brought the coffee and he drank it slowly out of one of the little cups which a hundred years ago an ancestor had brought from India. They were made not in India, but in China. India had only added the delicate silver filigree which formed the handle and decoration. India! How many of his ancestors had ruled there! But he had no desire to rule anybody. He set the cup down and went outside again into the sunshine. Bram had put the old terrace chairs outside and he lay down in one and closed his eyes and let the warmth seep through his veins like new blood. He didn't get enough sunshine. Perhaps no one got enough of it in England. Yet in Egypt during the war he had hated the hard hot light and he had dreamed of the cool shadows of the castle. Here the sunlight was mellow, penetrating mildly and without fever.

He lay motionless and thought of Betty Pound. What if he asked her and John down, say, for a weekend? No, they would be miserable and so would he. He'd run them down for a day. It would be long enough for him to see Betty moving about the place. The new and the old—the upstart young England forcing its way from hidden roots! What would John and Betty say when they saw the castle? He himself was young enough, but he did not belong in this new England. If he joined it of his own free will, it would mean effort, tearing down the past. He'd stand on his own, separated at last from his ancestors, and certainly his home could not be in a castle. The enormous problem of his life faced him again, and, thinking of Betty, he grew restless and could not lie basking on the terrace. She was so pretty a girl, not common or crude, not Cockney in the least. He'd never be ashamed of her here.

. . . To his surprise, they took a profound interest in the castle. He was accustomed to such interest, but he had not expected it from them. He was touched that they had even bought a small book about the place and knew the best pictures in the gallery and the names of the ancestral Monteiths in the portrait of Queen Elizabeth.

"A wonderful, clever, wicked face," Betty said musingly.

"Is it wicked?" Julian asked, smiling.

"Of course she was wicked." She flushed a little, but her lips closed firmly. "It makes people wicked to rule over others," she said.

"Ah well," he replied half in apology. "You see, she was born to it. She'd no choice."

"She could have just given it up when she found it was making her wicked," Betty said.

"Probably she didn't know it," Julian retorted.

"She knew," Betty said. "I can tell by the look in her green eyes. Let's go outside for a bit, Julian. I feel as if there were too many people here, all staring at me."

They went outside and wandered about until luncheon. He had thought of telling Bram not to make it too grand, then he had decided to let all happen as it would. Luncheon was served with splendor in the dining room. He was pleased that both John and Betty were neither overwhelmed nor ill at ease. They accepted Bram's ministrations and ate with good manners. Julian was slightly ashamed of himself that he had thought it might be otherwise.

John ate heartily. "I'm not used to country air," he said with a warm grin.

Betty ate little and she toyed with the fish on her plate.

Her face was rosy with sunburn and her short lashes were very black. Something of her gaiety was gone, Julian saw, but she was self-possessed, and when the talk wandered from the village near the castle to nationalized medicine she grew positive again.

"I do believe in common folk having the best," she declared.

John laughed. "That's because you and I belong to the common folk, maybe."

Betty flung back her curly black hair. "What if we do? It's not of us I'm thinking, though, John."

"She's right in that, Julian," John said, his mouth full of potato.

Julian had had at first a foolish feeling of shock when they began to call him Julian in the easy way of the young upon the streets. Then he had rather liked it, especially when they met in restaurants, or once in a way when they went boating and even once to the sea. Here in the castle he felt shocked again, and was disgusted that he did.

"Have an egg, Betty," he said. "You're tired of fish. Who isn't?"

"Do you have an egg?" she asked rather eagerly.

"We're lucky in having farms," he said mildly.

"I would like to see them," she said, still eagerly. "And I'd dearly like an egg."

So after the meal was over they sauntered down to the village and over the fields. Betty was quiet while she saw everything.

"Does it all belong to you, then, Julian?" she asked.

"I'm afraid so," Julian answered. He gave her a small smile. "It's far too much for one man, isn't it!"

"Wickedly much," she said quickly.

Now he laughed. "Still, I was born here, remember, quite innocently."

"Ah, but you won't be innocent if you keep it."

"Come, come!" he retorted, but with humor. They had reached a hillock and he sat down, and then they followed.

"Tell me, you two," he said, "what would you do—if you were I?"

John Pound looked at his sister and shook his head. "I don't know, Julian, and that's truth. The upkeep must be frightful."

"In the old way, impossible," Julian replied.

"I think a lot of people ought to enjoy it—and pay for it," Betty said decisively. She stared at the huge gray walls on the hill above them. "I don't see how anyone could feel it was a home."

"I do," Julian said. "Not just because it's mine, but because my family shares it with me, living and dead. I don't see where we are, exactly, in your England, Betty, but here we are. I don't suppose we'll be dispensed with—but I don't know."

"No fear," John Pound said heartily. But Betty said nothing. She continued to look at the castle with what Julian perceived now was a sort of heartbreak. Sensitive and quick-feeling, he saw clearly at this moment that she loved him and his heart grew soft indeed. If he loved her, he would reach out for her hand and tell her, through the touch of their fingers, that the castle was nothing. Her hand lay on the new green grass, half open, perhaps even waiting. But he continued to sit with his hands clenched about his knees.

John Pound felt uneasiness in the air and he rose briskly. "We ought to be thinking of the train, Bet," he said.

She rose, and the three of them began climbing the hill to the castle. "You'll have tea before you go?" Julian said, hating himself for the sudden coldness in his heart.

"We'll just get a cup at the station," Betty said.

"Do come in and rest a few minutes until the motor is here," Julian urged.

"I'd rather wait outside, please," she said.

So they waited outside, and when the motor came she put out her firm bare hand and touched his quickly.

"Thank you," she said. "Thank you very much. I understand

so many things now that I didn't before." Her eyes were dark and soft.

"I'm glad of that," Julian murmured. He was much taller than she was, and when he looked down he felt her small and infinitely human.

"You must come and have a bite with us," John Pound said heartily. "We'll serve it ourselves, Julian, but Betty is a good cook."

"I'm sure she's good at everything," Julian said, "and of course I'll come."

"Set the day, Betty," John urged.

She would not set the day. She shook her head, her cheeks bright. "I shan't know what I'll be doing next," she said positively.

John looked at her, surprised. "Now whatever does that mean?" he demanded.

"Just what it says," she retorted.

She lowered her lashes and began drawing on her brown cotton gloves quickly, but both men saw tears brimming on her red cheeks.

"Well, I never!" John exclaimed in simple consternation.

"Never mind," Julian said, "I quite understand."

He put an arm on the shoulder of each of them and walked with them to the door.

After they had gone the castle seemed welcoming. The great rooms opened one into another and he felt their endless repose. He needed it, for he suddenly felt tired, Somehow the day had been a strain, although they had been so nice, really, good and friendly. But Betty, dear little thing, had been lost. He saw that now. The castle had frowned at her and scared her.

"Beastly old thing," he muttered affectionately. He was stretched out in one of the old leather chairs in the library. He opened his eyes to glare about him, but when he did so the huge room enclosed him in warm dark shadows. Bram had made a fire, thinking he would serve their tea here. The lamps were low and the firelight moved in soft flashes over the backs of the gold-lettered books. He had read too few of them. When he was old, when he was very old, he would sit here and read them all.

"Here's your tea, sir," Bram said, coming in with a tray.

"Ah," he sighed, "that's good. Make it strong, please, Bram."

"Yes, sir," Bram said.

He took a holiday from London for a week and then two, and during these days he looked a good deal at Queen Elizabeth. The painter had caught her in one of her rare gay moods, and he did not think she looked wicked. Only prejudice could so have condemned her. The notion that Betty Pound might be prejudiced was a new one to him and he carried it about for a day or two while he rode over the farms and conversed with his manager about seed corn and young lambs. Was there perhaps a slight difference even in this man's behavior, something a little less than the deference he had used to breathe out whenever he was with his master? The possibility made Julian stiffen slightly as he turned his horse homeward.

At dinner, alone with Bram, he put a question to that unchanging soul. "Bram, would you say I'm as well liked as ever about the countryside?"

Bram coughed behind his hand. "Well, Your Lordship—I hardly know."

"Of course you know, Bram," Julian said brusquely. "Out with it, man! If you hedge, then I'll have my answer."

"If Your Lordship must 'ave it, sir, I should say Your Lordship is warmly liked—as a man."

"As a man—oh?" Julian said, half smiling. "But not as a lord, eh?"

"People seem to think lords are going out of fashion, so to speak," Bram said apologetically.

"Are we indeed!" Julian retorted.

"Not to me, sir, of course," Bram said hastily.

Julian ate the rest of his meal in silence. Bram was more than usually correct, and he did not offer a word, even with the wine. Alone with excellent port, Julian felt his anger rise and he did not repress it. Out of fashion! There was prejudice! He held his glass high, squinting at the brilliant vintage. "It's *our* England, too," he thought, and drank down his wine. It did not quench his rising rebellion. "I've a right to live, I hope," he told himself. "As good a right as any man!"

He thought suddenly of Lady Mary of Guilford, and how her hair had shone in the sun.

. . . Guilford Castle, he found, was just over the border of Sussex. This meant that it was in easy distance and explained why Lady Mary had been so casual about reaching Lydding-ton and getting home again the same day. But casualness was the air of the family. The Earl was digging in a vegetable garden when Julian arrived. He heard a high old voice answer the announcement of his coming with something like impatience. "Bring him here—can't you see I have my hands in the lettuces?"

"Yes, Your Lordship." the deprecating voice of the butler replied—the butler who in these peculiar times was several other men as well.

Julian, in his oldest and smallest motor, felt sorry for him when he returned through the misty warm atmosphere of that day.

"His Lordship is in the—kitchen garden, sir, and he'll receive you there. If you'll just follow, sir—"

So he had followed and had beheld the Earl rising from his knees, which were wet. "Hallo," the old gentleman said, holding out a muddied slender hand. "I don't know you."

"Nor I you, sir," Julian replied. "But I met your daughter rather accidentally several weeks ago and I thought I'd look her up. She was kind enough to tell me you lived here."

The Earl let his mouth hang ajar while he took this in. "Where do you come from?" he asked.

"I'm Monteith," Julian said simply.

"Oh, Monteith," the Earl repeated. "It was your father I knew in the days when I went up to London, I expect, unless it was your grandfather?"

"My father, I imagine, since I was at Oxford when your son was," Julian replied.

"Yes, I daresay," the Earl murmured. "He's not here now—while Parliament's sitting." His eyes wandered to a small heap of wilting lettuces. "Well, Mary must be about," he said vaguely.

"The writing room, Your Lordship," the butler murmured. In the brightening noon light small beads of sweat could be seen on his bald forehead. Clearly, he was uncomfortable at this meeting of peers in a vegetable garden.

"Take him there," the old Earl replied with relief, and went down on his knees again.

"If you'll follow me, please," the butler said, averting his eyes.

So Julian followed, to be halted at the garden gate by the Earl's voice, shouting, "Stay to luncheon, will you? It's a long-ish way otherwise."

"Thank you, sir," Julian called back.

He followed again, entering the castle by a path between hedges that led to a side door. He followed across a great library and to the open door of the writing room, where the butler, relieved, announced him very properly and then departed. He was left standing at the door, to meet the startled eyes of Lady Mary. She sat at a wide inlaid writing desk, her fair hair matching a bowl of pale jonquils upon it and her eyes very blue. He saw at once that her lower lip was inky, and when he went in and she put out her hand to him, her fingers, too, were inked.

"I hope you don't think it's too soon for me to look you up," he said, sitting down on a chair near her. "I suddenly felt very angry about something and I wanted to see you at once."

She was wearing a soft blue wool frock and she sat looking at him in a dreamy silence.

"Do I disturb you?" he asked.

"I'm only writing something," she said a little breathlessly. "It doesn't matter."

Her eyes were sweet and he saw that she was shy. This he had not understood when he had seen her before.

"What do you write?" he asked.

"It's a story," she replied unwillingly.

"About?" he hinted.

"Someone—rather like myself."

"Then it must be interesting," he said.

"It isn't really about me," she went on reluctantly. "It's about—England."

"Ah," he said. "That's what I came to see you for."

Her left hand, hanging over the edge of the chair, was long and lovely, delicate as a lily, but now a little roughened and he saw the nail of the forefinger was broken.

"Is there any place in England for us?" he asked directly.

"Us?" she repeated.

"People in castles—remember?"

She sat looking at him, her eyes still dreaming. "Yes!" she said softly. "Because we are good!"

The simplicity of this answer confounded him. He sat slackly, gazing at her. Then he remembered Queen Elizabeth and Betty Pound and shook his head. "It's very hard for people nowadays to believe that we can be good."

She pushed her chair back at that and walked across the wide room to the window that overlooked a hillside and a river, and he watched her as she moved and as she stood. Here in the place where she had been born and had grown up she was beautiful. Love and grace had gone to make her. She had been nursed on beauty, and space became her. Deep and distant voices cried out in his blood and his heart stirred.

"But we know we are good," she said clearly. "We have a right to live—surely, surely! If we live for England—"

"For England made us," he said gravely.

Slowly the world in which they lived became their own again, the world in which castles had their place, too, among the homes of men.

But of course he could not hurry her. They had time ahead,

time in which to meet, to talk, to walk together, to learn to speak their private names to each other. Hundreds of years were behind them, hundreds of years ahead. He was profoundly glad that he had obeyed his father—he had not wasted himself.

She turned her pure blue eyes to him. "Would you like to see the castle?" she asked.

"Nothing would make me happier," he replied.

Pleasant Evening

It was a pleasant evening. After the long winter the cold had broken and Elaine had opened the window near which she sat. The mild sweet air of spring flowed into the heated room, and the other guests turned gratefully toward her. Even Ruth, her hostess, smiled.

"We are letting ourselves argue too much," she said. "I'm going to get something cool to drink."

She rose gracefully and went out, and Matt Buell, her husband, passed cigarettes. To take one, light it, and begin to smoke gave them all a chance to pause and search for calm again. The room was rather small, and it had suddenly seemed too full. Actually, there was plenty of room for six people—Elaine and Bart, Matt and Ruth, and Wilson and his wife. The Wilsons were middle-aged, enough older so that the other four had deferred to them until they disagreed. Then they had all divided into argument. Wilson was the dean of the university and Matt was head of the department where Elaine and Bart were graduate students. Bart was working with U-235 and she was working with radioactive isotopes. Bart called it all The Stuff. Bart was Ruth's younger brother, and he and Elaine were engaged.

She was proud of Bart. Slim and tall, his thin face pale against his dark hair, only he had been calm throughout. He had said very little, listening with a slight smile on his lips to Matt and the dean arguing against Ruth and Mrs. Wilson. Once he had said, "But we are living *now*, Mrs. Wilson. It's a different age, not so pleasant as the one into which you were born. Yet it is the only one we have."

Mrs. Wilson's kind plain face had flushed. "What troubles me is that you young people are so mild. You accept everything. When I was young, if we didn't like something we changed it."

Elaine's heart had flown to Bart. "Pity you didn't change enough so that we don't have to live in this kind of a world!" These were the words that had risen to her lips. But she had not spoken them. There was no use in talking to old people—she shared this belief firmly with her generation. Bart said there was no use in talking to old people. She had seen the smile on his lips deepen. That meant he was thinking the same thing. He would say no more. It was at this moment that she had thrown open the window.

Ruth came in with a tray of tall glasses, lemon juice and sugar, gin and ice. "It's really turned too warm," she said gaily. "It isn't just us."

Matt got up and began to mix drinks, taking it for granted that everybody was thirsty. "I'll have just water, please," Mrs. Wilson said.

"Plenty of gin for me," Bart murmured.

They took their glasses and sipped the cool stuff. The spring air flowed in upon them, vaguely fragrant with poplar and willow blossoms. Elaine leaned on the windowsill and looked out into the soft darkness. Children had been playing outside when they came in from the dinner table, but long ago had gone to bed. Across the wide quiet street she saw a man and his wife sitting beside a lamp on a table. The man was reading and the woman was sewing. A pot of bright flowers stood under the lamp. It was too far away to see what they were. The surrounding darkness made the scene a picture of peace. She could imagine every room in the house. Upstairs, children were sleeping. Someday she and Bart would sit like that beside a lighted lamp in their own house, and upstairs their children would be sleeping. She turned her head and looked at him with love. He had set down his glass and he was smoking slowly and deeply, his pale face still set in a smile, his dark eyes absently staring at nothing. So much of the time he seemed to be staring at nothing, his lids dropped, his head bent. That was the way he sat in class, as though he heard nothing. But she knew he heard everything. Afterward in lab he used everything he had heard and went straight on deducing from what he already knew. Last December he had discovered a reagent which released a new by-product of U-235, and he had won the Brownell Award. He had taken half the money to buy her a huge yellow diamond for her engagement ring. She had never seen a yellow diamond, but he had insisted that it was the only stone possible for her dark red hair and brown eyes. When he had put it on her finger she had known he was right.

She was glad that she was intelligent enough to be his wife. Quite coldly she knew she was. An ordinary girl would have been crushed by him. Not that he would have been consciously cruel—yes, perhaps he would have been. But she could trust her own good brain to deal with him. She knew he loved her, and her own love for him was the breath of her life and the beat of her heart. But she knew as much as he did, she was as daring as he was, if not so spectacular. She had always to prove every step of her work as she went, check and countercheck, while he went soaring on, checking nothing, guided only by his matchless flair. They were a good pair, she with her prudence and competence, he with his flair. They had mutual pride in one another's work and he did not want her to stop working when they were married.

"Lord, no!" he had laughed yesterday when she asked him. "I don't want to marry a housewife! The world's too full of them."

They had been walking through an empty campus. Everybody else had gone home. It was twilight. They had walked along hand in hand. It had been a little cold yesterday, and she had buttoned her coat around her throat and let the wind blow back her hair. Then, feeling his eyes on her, she had turned and met his gaze, very steady and firm. When he did look directly, his eyes were piercing.

"When are we going to get married?" he had asked.

"June?" she suggested. "I believe it's supposed to be the best month. I'll be finished this project of mine by the first, I think. I'd like to have it off my mind."

"June the second, then," he said. "No big wedding, of course."

"Not exactly of course, but all right," she conceded.

"Here," he said next, "we'll just knock off work and do it."

"My family won't like that," she said doubtfully.

"I've always wanted a private wedding," he replied. "Matt and Ruth will stand up with us."

She put away the thought of her father and mother and sister at home in Wisconsin. Bart had not met them. He had insisted on waiting until after they were married, when nothing could be done about it. For the same reason he had not taken her to his own home in Philadelphia. "Let them lump us," he had said.

He had called Ruth at once and Ruth had invited her to dinner tonight, even though the dean and his wife were already coming. "We can talk about the wedding after they've gone," she had said comfortably.

It did not look as though the Wilsons were ever going. Mrs. Wilson looked wistfully at Bart, who did not look up. She was yearning over him, seeing, Elaine supposed, something of the son she had lost in the war; an only child, Robert had been. He had not been decently killed. Instead he had been taken in the Battle of the Bulge and had died of starvation and beating. Dean Wilson had written a letter to the newspaper, for the sake of their friends, so that they would know about Bob, he said, and then the story would not have to be told again and again. Elaine had only seen Bob a few times. He looked like any other undergraduate, and he was not handsome because he looked too much like his mother.

Bob was captured in December and taken with others to a military prison in Germany, Dean Wilson had written. Some contractor wanted more workers, and about two hundred Americans, Bob with them, were sent in a locked cattle car to Thuringia. It took ten days. There great caverns were being dug in the rocky hillside to be used as workshops for the making of instruments of war, and Bob with others was put to shoveling broken rock into cars. The daily ration for the heavy work was one pan of watery soup and one slice of bread. The prisoners could not live very long on this and they were not expected to live. The plan was to get as much work out of them as possible before they died. When they faltered they were beaten. Clubs, weighted metal hose, and rifle butts were used, and the sick were driven to work at the point of a bayonet. Bob grew weak and slowed up and was beaten until at last he got it every day. There was no medical attention. His weight dropped from one hundred and sixty-five pounds to eighty pounds. On June 2, 1945, his twenty-second birthday, he died. That was the end of Dean Wilson's letter.

Elaine thought of it now as she looked at Mrs. Wilson. Tears came into her eyes, but Mrs. Wilson did not see them. She was still looking at Bart with her wistful gray gaze. She began to speak softly, gently. "You are right in what you say, Bart. This is the only world you have. I know it's partly our fault. We didn't see it coming. I don't know why—it happened so suddenly. It seemed such a pleasant good world, it seemed easy to change what we didn't like. There was so much good-

ness when I was a girl. I remember even men like old Andrew
Carnegie seemed to be good—putting libraries everywhere,
you know."

Bart lifted his head and stared at her with strange hostile
eyes. Then he threw back his head and gave a loud bark of
laughter. The next instant he was sober again. "Excuse me,"
he said, and dropped his eyes.

Mrs. Wilson looked bewildered, but she went on. "I don't
know when this dreadful new world began," she said. Her
voice quivered.

"Oh, I hope she doesn't speak of Bob," Elaine thought.
"Bart won't bear that."

But Mrs. Wilson did not speak of Bob. No one had ever
heard her speak of Bob since the letter was published in the
newspaper. No one had spoken to her of him after that. She
went on in her quivering gentle voice, struggling to be calm.
"If we older ones had understood, we might have done something. But we didn't know what was going on underneath
the pleasant surface. Now, of course, the surface is gone. We
don't know what to do. We don't even know how to live in
this raw place where there is no surface any more. I just
keep—marking time, sort of, until I die." She could not control
two tears which now rolled down her cheeks, but she ignored
them. She did not put up her hand to wipe them away and
they fell on her bosom. They were all listening to her, not
looking at her, except Elaine, who could not look away. She
was thinking with Mrs. Wilson. Bob had been a baby, a little
boy, a big boy—she could see all the pictures of him now
going through Mrs. Wilson's mind.

Mrs. Wilson was still talking in a pleading voice. "You're
scientists, Bart—you and Elaine. Couldn't you young scientists
sort of refuse to—to make things they could use for war?
Because I don't see how else it's ever going to be stopped.
And they're dependent on you—if you don't show them how
to kill people, they won't know how to do it—in millions, I
mean."

It was a foolish and pitiful plea. Dean Wilson cleared his throat and tried to speak calmly. "What Mrs. Wilson means is what I've often thought. Hitler would have remained a beerhall character if tycoons had not backed his sadistic schemes—and if scientists had not made them weapons—"

"The atomic bomb!" Mrs. Wilson urged breathlessly.

Bart uncrossed his legs, sat up, drank the last of his cool drink, and lifted his head. His movements were sharp and his words brusque, the way they were in the laboratory. "It's scarcely fair to blame us for what's been going on for hundreds of years," he said. "Where will you lay the blame, Mrs. Wilson? Men began to study fission in India two thousand years ago. Ancient Egypt knew something about it. Each generation has stood upon the last one's shoulders. Will you blame Madame Curie because she discovered the use for radium? Will you damn Einstein because he set down on paper a formula which has helped us enormously? Just which scientist will you blame, Mrs. Wilson?"

Of course he was right, Elaine told herself. It would be the end of human progress if science was stopped in its eternal search.

Mrs. Wilson tried again feebly. "But it was so terrible the way that young man said he didn't feel anything when he dropped the bomb—even though he knew thousands of people would be killed!"

"Why should he feel anything, Mrs. Wilson?" Bart asked. "It was not his responsibility. He was only doing what he had been told to do. Blame his officer, if you like, who commanded him, yet he, too, was only obeying orders."

"Oh, Mrs. Wilson, stop!" Elaine cried in her heart. "You can't understand, poor dear. You're too old—and too sad." But she was silent.

Mrs. Wilson tried again. "But, Bart, that's what the Nazis say when we ask them why they did such terrible things. They say they had to—because it was orders."

"Then they are right," Bart said.

"Right to—to—" Mrs. Wilson asked wildly.

"Right to obey orders," Bart said.

Mrs. Wilson got up and her husband hastened to her side. She did not try to stop her crying now. "But why," she asked him, not knowing what she said, "why did we have Bob at all? We ought never to have let him be born!"

"Excuse us," Dean Wilson said. "She's not well. You'll understand—I'd better take her home."

They all got up, Bart standing up, too, very straight and still, the half-smile on his lips again. Matt and Ruth went out to the hall and he was left alone with Elaine.

"Whew!" he said, whistling through his teeth. "The older generation, muddling along!"

He went over to Elaine and put his forefinger under her chin. "Stay young, my sweet," he commanded her and he kissed her lightly on the lips.

They leaned together out of the window and the air was sweet and dark. "Let's skip," Bart said. "You and I. Matt and Ruth won't mind. We can talk later."

So they stole out of the room through the dining room and out by the kitchen door into the big back yard. Down at the far end was a grape arbor. The new leaves were unfolding and, although they could not be seen, Elaine with her delicate perception of fragrance could smell them, or she fancied she did. There was dew on the benches and Bart put his handkerchief down for her to sit upon, and when she sat down he put his arm around her and drew her close. He was an artist in making love and he savored every stage, never in haste, always fastidious. He kissed her hair, her eyebrows, the point of her chin, the bones of her cheeks, and at last her lips. She knew that he liked her to remain passive until the end.

But when he had kissed her lips, he suddenly took away his arm. "By the way, there's something I want to say." His voice was abrupt as though they had not just kissed each other.

She put back her tumbled hair. "Yes, Bart?"

"Look, kid, I want you to quit The Stuff."

She was bewildered by the sharpness in his voice. "But, Bart—I shan't be through for another two months!"

"I know—and that's what worries me. I was talking with old Wilson. His wife's a fool, but he isn't. He's right up to date on fission, I can tell you. And he said something today when he was looking at my report."

Dean Wilson was keeping daily check on Bart's experiments, she knew. He expected Bart would make the university famous someday, not too far off.

"Yes, Bart?"

"He said no one knew what might happen exactly to people who were working on The Stuff. Women especially."

"You mean—?"

"The Stuff might do something to your precious organs. We want to have kids, don't we?"

Children sleeping upstairs in the lamplit house! "Of course, Bart. That's the big dream."

"Well! So you quit, see?"

"But I have to do my work, Bart," she said steadily.

He would understand that. The glory of their love was that he held her equal to him. Her vocation for their work was the same as his.

"Sure you have to work, kid," he said kindly. "But at something else, please! For all our sakes."

"What about you?" She was surprised to hear how hostile her voice was.

"I'm more—protectable."

She did not speak. She could not. Home or career! The stale old cry of a past generation reared its defunct head in this strange new guise. She had to choose between the work which was her life, exactly as it was Bart's, and the chance that she might not be able to make a home. She had always taken it for granted, as a modern woman living in enlightened times, that she could and would have both.

"It's nature for a woman to want a home," her mother had complained when she heard that Elaine was going on working after she married. "You can't make a home if you're not in it—no woman can."

"I can, Mother," she had answered gaily. "Bart and I are going to beat nature, see?"

Maybe they couldn't. In her blind old-fashioned way maybe her mother was right.

"There are lots of other things you can do, honey," Bart said tenderly. "Everything's open to women nowadays."

"But I'm trained to work on The Stuff," she said. "It'll be dull to work on something else, Bart, and you know it."

He did know it. The Stuff was the fad now. Every young scientist took it as a matter of course that he would work with it. That was where the future lay, her future as well as his. She did not want to work at something else. She wanted to work at her job, the thing for which she was trained. She was a scientist to the bone, as much as Bart was. There had to be a way for her to be herself.

She felt the damp of dew settling upon her feet. The ground held the chill of winter, after all. "Bart, if it were you who was being told that we might not be able to have children if you kept on at your job, would you give up?"

He was silent for a moment. Then he reached into his pocket and drew out his pipe and tobacco. It was what he always did when he wanted time to think. He liked cigarettes better, but they gave him too little time. He filled his pipe and lit it with the lighter she had bought him for his birthday. He took plenty of time. When he spoke his voice was very calm. "That's unnecessary, isn't it? I mean, the facts are that I don't have to think about it."

Yes, he was right. She knew he was always scrupulously just, with a liberality which never held her lesser than he for being a woman. He had for her a consideration which her father had never given to her mother, for all his devotion, and which she knew Dean Wilson never gave poor Mrs. Wilson. It was literal and true that it was foolish to ask him to face a dilemma which he did not really have to face, and could not face, because it was not his. It was hers only. Men could take her place at the laboratory table, but no man could take her place in life. She was a woman, and she alone could bear children—Bart's children and hers.

"So I suppose I'm to be put back into my place," she said bitterly.

"I have an idea how you feel," Bart said with real tenderness. "I wish I knew a way out. Of course, we could forget the kids."

They knew they could not. Anyway, it was no solution. With her long years of training in science her mind sprang to the pinnacle of the universal. What was happening to her would happen to many women, potentially even to all. She was only one among millions. It might be possible for her to live as a scientist alone, without children, but could that be a solution?

Besides, she wanted children. "I want children, Bart," she said and felt her voice quiver exactly as Mrs. Wilson's had done.

"So do I," Bart said. "That's why I'm telling you this."

"I don't think I'll be happy to give up the job either, though, Bart."

"Looks like I'm going to have an unhappy wife no matter what happens," he said, trying to joke.

He smoked hard for a moment and she saw through the darkness the glow of his pipe bowl. "Don't try to decide tonight," he said suddenly. "You're tired. Let's let things ride, shall we? Skate along for a bit?"

It was his habitual conclusion to anything difficult. She felt the unconscious shrug of his shoulder against hers which always accompanied the words. Skate along! Skate over the potential horrors of what they were doing, skate over the possibilities of annihilation and devastation, even over the end of the world! The memories of old bull sessions in college rose to her mind. After Hiroshima there had been endless bull sessions. They didn't have them any more. They knew too much. They just skated along. She suddenly burned with anger against Bart because she wanted to cry and it was folly to cry. But she couldn't help it. She began to sob. He threw his pipe on the ground and turned to her.

"Elaine, what is this, darling? What have I done?"

She hated him with all her soul and she could not bear his touch. He was not Bart. He was only a man whom she hated.

"Don't touch me!" she cried.

"Elaine!"

"Let me go—"

She pulled herself out of his arms. She got up and stood trembling against the grapevines and all the time she went on crying out loud and could not stop. Her life was crumbling about her. For of course she had to have children. She could not live without love and home and children. But how could she live without herself and her work? How could she be happy while Bart went on and on without her? She would forget the very names of things, the immutable laws would slip from her dulled memory. She would become nothing. And her children would hate her. The children of Bart would despise her. And she could teach them nothing because she would know nothing. She could not answer even the question she asked of herself: "How shall I live?"

Bart was sitting very still. He had picked up his pipe and lit it. She could see the coal of tobacco glowing and in the glow as he drew hard on the pipe she saw his sharp handsome face light up and grow dark again. It looked cold and remote. Her sobbing died and she began to shiver with cold. She wanted to wound him very much because he was a man and he could not understand what it was to be a woman. She thought of Mrs. Wilson, whom Bart despised.

"Mrs. Wilson was right," she said between chattering teeth. "She was right when she said she ought not to have let Bob be born. Maybe I'd better not have any children either. Maybe the very Stuff you're working on will kill them anyway—in bombs."

"Don't be silly," he said shortly.

"You can't promise me it won't, can you?" she demanded. Her voice was shrill and she could not help it. "Look, here's a bargain, Bart—I'll give up if you will. See, it's fair, isn't it? You say The Stuff may throw off rays that will kill the kids before they're born. I say The Stuff may kill them after they're born. So let's both give up, Bart. Then they can live, maybe."

"I will not listen to such nonsense," Bart said. He got up, knocked the ash from his pipe. "I never knew you to be hysterical. I guess you're tired. Come along—I'm going to see that you get to your door safely. We'll think this over for a few days."

They had both forgotten they were going to talk about the wedding. He reached for her and pulled her away from the grapevines. "Why, you are cold as ice, you idiot!"

She did not protest. She let him take her to the car and push her in and they rattled down the street to her dormitory. The sky was glorious with stars. They had opened like flowers in the warm night. They were not brilliant like the winter stars prickling with cold. They burned soft and deep in the sky.

She did not speak. It was only a matter of minutes until he drew up at the door and helped her out. He gave her a long hard kiss before he opened the door. It was so late that the lights were out in the windows. "You get to sleep in a hurry," he commanded. "Don't lie awake. Forget everything, will you, kid? Everybody can have kids, but not everybody can make The Stuff, eh? Maybe that's the way it'll happen. Anyway, we'll just skate along, eh?"

"Maybe," she said dully.

She kissed him back, making effort enough so that he would say no more, would go away and leave her alone. Then she went upstairs slowly to her small single room and undressed and washed and went to bed. "Just skate along," he'd said, even about this. But skate over what—to what? Suddenly she buried her face in the pillow. She saw Bob in the cave. She wanted to cry about Bob because he'd been beaten to death. Bob—poor Bob! She began to cry terribly as if she could never stop.

The Three Daughters

Muriel Reynolds was waiting for her half-sister Joanna. They had agreed to meet for luncheon in this small French restaurant uptown, to discuss the fate of their third sister, Priscilla, who was half-sister to them both. Priscilla was still a child, nine years of age, while they were grown, Muriel six years older than Joanna, who was only twenty. At twenty-six Muriel had a responsible position on a fashion magazine and Joanna looked up to her, while keeping a mind of her own.

The three daughters of Morgan Reynolds were close friends, occasionally brief enemies, and always united in their common possession, their father. They had never lived together, for their mothers were all different women and one by one had divorced Morgan, so that now he lived alone in the big brownstone house, where, daughter by daughter, singly and never together, the three girls visited him during vacations or weekly, as the judge had decided, as long as they were minors. Muriel, being grown, visited him when she wished and when it was convenient for him, which was not often, because she reminded him of her mother. Joanna had one more month to spend with him in the coming summer before she was twenty-one. Priscilla spent each Saturday with him.

Today was Saturday and Muriel knew that, the day being fine, her father and Priscilla were wandering about the park, hand in hand, feeding the animals in the zoo and buying themselves the poisonous refreshments in which she herself had once delighted when it had been her turn to wander with him through the park. On rainy days he took his daughters to the movies or, if he was serious, to a museum, where he explained to them the principles of art.

Muriel glanced at her small wristwatch. Joanna was late as usual, although Muriel had made her promise she would not eat breakfast at her mother's apartment but would come here and have scrambled eggs while Muriel herself had a lamb chop. She had ordered the luncheon and she was hungry, but she would not begin. She was punctilious, a thin, rather angular young woman, and she knew she was not her father's favorite daughter. She had been aware of this all the time that Joanna was growing up, and now they both knew that Priscilla was the favorite. She had been able to help Joanna a good deal when their father married again and Priscilla was born and took Joanna's place.

"He never seems to have room for more than one at a time," Joanna had mourned.

She saw Joanna now, on tiptoe, searching the crowded tables to find her, the two little scarlet wings on her hat fluttering this way and that. She waved her napkin and Joanna saw her and came toward her. She was looking pretty, Muriel saw at once, for she had inherited the dark prettiness of her mother, just as Muriel had inherited her own mother's red hair and gray eyes. Priscilla was a golden blonde.

"I don't know why I can't wake up on Saturdays," Joanna complained.

"Did you eat breakfast?" Muriel demanded.

"No, I didn't, I promise, only a cup of coffee," Joanna said.

"I've ordered," Muriel said. She nodded at the waiter and

he set on the table two large glasses of orange juice.

"Haven't you had your breakfast?" Joanna asked.

"Ages ago. I'm having luncheon," Muriel said briefly. "How much did you pay for that dress?"

"Thirty-nine fifty."

"That's high. It's good-looking, though."

"I shan't need another until summer."

They were both thinking the same thing. The alimony always ran short for her mother. Muriel was earning her own way and her mother was getting along comfortably now, but Joanna's mother was extravagant by nature. Their father had joked about that a good deal. "I had to divorce Jill because it was too expensive to be her husband. It's cheaper to pay her alimony." The lawyers had made a very tight arrangement, at his request. That was the way he was—he joked about something to everybody, but by himself he was very sharp.

The eggs and lamb chop appeared and the waiter poured coffee.

"Do you want to talk now or shall we just eat?" Joanna asked.

Muriel looked at her watch again—it was a nervous habit like a tic. "I don't want to hurry you."

"Oh, I shan't hurry," Joanna said cheerfully.

"Well, suppose you tell me what you have seen," Muriel suggested. She cut her meat small and ate neatly and quickly. Her mother was a high-tempered handsome woman, and she had taught Muriel to be absolutely obedient. Sometimes she had whipped her. They might have hated each other, but they did not because they had to stay together. There was no one else. When Muriel came home from her visits to her father, her mother would not ask her a question or allow her to mention his name. This, Muriel knew, was entirely different from Joanna's mother, who wanted to know all about him. She knew because she and Joanna talked over everything. Had they not shared their father, she doubted whether they would ever have been friends, they were so different, but as it was they carried on a curious triangular family life. Her mother would not meet Joanna's mother, who had displaced her, but they both knew and liked Priscilla's mother, Jennie, who was a gentle yellow-haired woman with soft violet eyes.

"I know your father is a fiend," Muriel's mother had said, "but I really cannot understand why even he should divorce Jennie. Anyone could get on with her."

Jennie herself did not understand. She was humble about it and said that Morgan was so brilliant that he was bored with her.

Joanna's mother had shrieked laughter at this naïveté. "Morgan has the habit of divorce now," she declared. "He can't think of anything else to do. It doesn't occur to him to put himself out."

"Well," Joanna said now, surreptitiously dunking a bit of hard roll in her coffee, "I first saw her in the park with him. He had asked me to come and fetch Priscilla that Saturday afternoon because he was busy and couldn't spend his usual time with her. If it was rainy I was to meet them under the Venus de Milo in the museum, and if it wasn't I was to meet them in the monkey house. Well, Priscilla was in the monkey house by herself, and he was outside talking to a woman."

"I wonder if it was the same one I saw," Muriel said, reflecting.

"Not at all pretty," Joanna said.

"Not ugly," Muriel suggested.

"No," Joanna agreed, "but not what he usually wants."

The three mothers were all pretty, and Muriel's mother must, Muriel often thought, have been a real beauty at first, a statuesque tall girl, a little taller than her father. Joanna's mother, by contrast, was very small, a picturesque untidy woman, always curling up in the corner of a chair or a sofa. By instinct she chose the largest piece of furniture in the room, where she looked like a gay mouse.

"She looked competent," Joanna said.

"That wouldn't be too bad," Muriel said. "But we must think of Priscilla. She is younger even than I was when the divorce came."

She wished now that she had looked more carefully at the woman she had seen with her father that rainy day when she happened upon them walking down Fifth Avenue together under his large black umbrella. She had recognized her father's English shoes and his gray ulster although beside them were a neat pair of galoshes on rather small feet tripping along under a circular skirt of brown cloth.

The umbrella lifted as she passed and she saw her father's startled face. "Oh, it's you, Muriel," he said by way of greeting.

"Hello, Dad," she said, and then she saw that the woman's hand was tucked into her father's elbow with a gesture which was familiar if not downright clinging. She looked into a surprised rosy face, wholesome and not pretty except that the mouth was nice.

Her father mumbled something and she had gone on.

"The question is," she now said to Joanna, "do we want a fourth in the family? Priscilla is hopelessly mixed up as it is."

"Can we help it?" Joanna countered. "He has always done what he wanted."

"We have to think of Priscilla," Muriel persisted. "It has been a struggle to get you educated, and she is only nine. The woman looked a fertile kind of creature, don't you think? She might even have twins. And can he pay another alimony? After all, he's fifty-four. Jennie says she doesn't know whether he has anything in his will for Priscilla. He's no millionaire, you know."

"No, but he can earn money whenever he works," Joanna said. "All he has to do is to stay at the office."

Morgan Reynolds was an advertising genius, and it was true that when he wrote copy for any firm the dollars flowed toward him. He had grown apathetic about his gifts as he grew older. Alimony was an easy way to spend money, he said, so easy it was scarcely worth while to make it at all, except that grim law waited like a tiger to pounce upon him. It was still the male who paid and paid, he declared.

"I feel sorry for him," Muriel said suddenly. "He's really got very little for his money."

"Whose fault is that?" Joanna asked. "My mother didn't want a divorce. She always says she didn't mind him and wouldn't mind him today. He was the one. He just kept saying, 'Go to hell,' no matter what she asked him."

"What did she ask him?" Muriel inquired.

"Nothing unusual, she says. Just things that women always ask, like will you be late for dinner tonight and do you think we can go to Florida next winter, or she needed money. One day he said he couldn't stand it and he wanted a divorce, but to this day she doesn't know what it was that he couldn't stand. Does *your* mother?"

"My mother couldn't stand *him,*" Muriel said. "She has a temper and he has a temper and neither one would give in. I remember once they didn't speak for more than six months. They both talked to me, and I had to tell the other one. It was wearing."

"Why did they finally speak?" Joanna asked.

"Mother said she had to tell him she wanted a divorce and he said, 'Good, why didn't I think of it first?' After that they talked and things were better."

"But they still got the divorce."

"Oh, yes, it was the only thing to do. Even I could see that."

"Has she never regretted it?"

"No, she hasn't. She hasn't even wanted to get married again. That's one trouble about him. None of them want to marry again after he's been their husband."

"Oh, of course he's fearfully charming," Joanna said.

"If charm is what you want," Muriel agreed. "I don't care for it myself."

They sat back for the waiter to take away their plates and bring desserts. Joanna wanted dessert, a slice of cherry pie even if it was breakfast. Muriel chose pastry. She could eat anything and stay thin, like her mother. Joanna had to be careful. Her mother had to be careful too, and that was one thing she always said that Morgan could not hold up against her. She had not lost her figure before the divorce.

"Well, this doesn't get us anywhere," Muriel said when she had finished. "Do you think we ought to pump Priscilla for information?"

They were both fond of Priscilla and one or the other of them usually took her to Sunday school and church because Jennie slept late.

"It's my turn tomorrow," Muriel went on. "I could ask her."

"What?" Joanna demanded.

"Well, whether there's a lady sometimes, for instance."

"Mean, isn't it?" Joanna said reluctantly.

"What do you suggest, then?" Muriel asked, a little on edge.

"I have nothing to suggest," Joanna said.

"Well," Muriel retorted.

They paid, each for what she ate, and parted.

The next morning Muriel got up early as usual and dressed herself carefully for church. As soon as she had eaten her breakfast she went to fetch Priscilla, who would be waiting and ready except for the details of inspection. She was a good little thing and long ago had learned not to trouble her mother.

She was just finishing a bowl of breakfast food when Muriel came in, using the latchkey which Jennie had given her so she need not be wakened.

"Hello, Prissy," Muriel said. "Wipe the milk off your mouth, and let's go. Do you have your dime and nickel?"

The dime was for Sunday school and the nickel for church. Occasionally Priscilla changed and kept the dime for church.

"Mother forgot," she said.

"Never mind, I have some extras," Muriel said cheerfully.

She bent and kissed her half-sister's round cheek. "You smell nice."

"I used some of Mother's perfume," Priscilla said. She liked Muriel best for several things and Joanna best for others. Joanna played better, but Muriel was better to go to church with.

"Did you have a nice time yesterday?" Muriel asked. The day was fine and they walked as usual, Priscilla skipping a bit now and then.

"I had a lovely time," Priscilla said. "Miss Markham came and she and Daddy were busy and so we didn't go to the park. I used up all the records and I played all the ones I like best lots of times over."

"Who is Miss Markham?" Muriel asked.

"She's Daddy's best friend," Priscilla said. "She's nice, I like her. She talks to me."

"Is she always at his house when you are?" Muriel asked.

"Most always," Priscilla said. "I asked her if Daddy was going to marry her and she said she hadn't decided."

"And what were they busy at?" Muriel asked, her blood chilling.

"Talking and talking," Priscilla said.

"Was the door shut?" Muriel asked.

"It was open and then it was shut," the child replied.

The church was unfortunately near and there was no time to put further questions, but these were enough. Muriel went through the rituals of the morning without hearing what the rector said. Even the music seemed distant. She was pondering upon her father, that man who disliked women and yet somehow had gathered about himself six women, wives and daughters, and was now contemplating a seventh. How could this be explained, and not only the man but the women? They who were the daughters were scarcely to blame and yet she felt responsible for him because he had bestowed life upon her, unwittingly and perhaps unwillingly. She herself would have been glad not to be born, she saw no great benefit in life as it appeared to a woman today, especially a young one, and yet nevertheless she was here, a tall, ascetic, slightly acid-looking young woman, as she very well knew, with all sorts of restrained impulses and emotions. The only tenderness she felt was toward Joanna and Priscilla. She loved them and she would take care of them as long as she lived, even if they did not need her. Her mother's bitter tongue had never spared her, though in their curious way they were fond of each other, but her mother did not need love and there was no use in wasting it upon her.

Priscilla was different. Sitting in the hard church pew, Muriel looked down at her small sister's profile and felt her heart melt at the sight of that tender outline. Priscilla was too trusting; she believed everybody and she must be protected without destroying the trust. Muriel, trusting no one, could appreciate nevertheless that bloom of faith.

Here in the church where the atmosphere was mild with goodness she determined to do her duty with love. She would go and talk with her father this very night.

"Well," Morgan Reynolds said on the Sunday evening. "What brings you here, Muriel?"

He was alone in the house. The servants were off and he was trying to decide whether he would remain alone or whether he would call up Angela Markham and suggest a drive into the country. Then the doorbell rang and he went to the door and discovered his eldest daughter on the threshold.

"I thought you might be at home," Muriel said. "I want to talk with you."

"Talk," Morgan grumbled, and he led her, his arm through hers, into the living room. "Your mother was always wanting to talk with me."

"I am sorry I remind you of her, Dad," Muriel said. "I suppose I can't help it. Anyway, what I want to say now has nothing to do with her."

Morgan liked this downright and somewhat angular daughter. Of the three of them, he had always in the back of his mind that he might invite Muriel here someday to live with him, providing that her mother would be so kind as to die, which he did not expect. Women like Marcella lived forever. They fed on their tempers: rage was their source of vitality.

"I suppose you've eaten something," he said. "The servants left that plate of sandwiches and the thermos of coffee. It's my usual Sunday supper when they're gallivanting."

"Thank you, I'd like some," Muriel said. She helped herself heartily and he approved her appetite. If there was anything he hated, it was a woman who talked about her diet the way Jill always had. He sat down and watched her eat.

"Good!" he said. "Go to it. I like to see it."

"I want to talk to you about Priscilla," Muriel said.

His good humor made him approve her looks tonight; the severe gray suit, the little green hat were becoming. "Priscilla is all right. She was here yesterday."

"I know she was," Muriel said. She was not shy or embarrassed. "I asked her what she did and she said Miss Markham was here. Dad, I don't think you ought to carry on right before her."

"What do you mean, 'carry on'?" Morgan demanded. "You sound like your mother again."

"I'm not like her, though," Muriel said. "I don't care what you do for your own pleasure, but I don't think Priscilla ought to be here. Besides, Dad, it's ridiculous. Four!"

"There's no fourth as yet," he declared.

"Well, we know the signs. We are concerned."

"Who's concerned?"

"Joanna and I are."

"What business is it of yours?"

He tried to get out something about its not being anybody's damned business, but she would have none of it. "Oh, yes, it is. We're the daughters. And how can you manage still another alimony, Dad?"

"Alimony!" he shouted. "I'm not married yet."

"But—"

"Shut up," he said. He knew what she meant to say and she did not have to go on.

Then he melted, his soft interior always overcoming him, and he apologized in his own way. "I am so damned lonely here sometimes—not all the time, but sometimes. Tonight is one of them."

"Your own fault, isn't it?" she suggested.

"Yes and no," he said. "If your three mothers could have been all in one, I'd have managed. They were too single-minded, there was no change. You won't believe me, you hard-hearted virgin, but the truth is I've missed them all in one way and been damned glad I was rid of them in others. I need variety, and I hate being promiscuous. That's what made me marry one after the other instead of just—"

He broke off. After all, she was his daughter.

"What makes you think that Miss Markham is a package?" Muriel asked.

He wanted to show a paternal indignation at this cynicism, but instead his humor got the better of him and he laughed. "I don't know," he confessed. "I just find myself hoping."

Muriel looked at him thoughtfully, a pleasant sight, she had to admit, his gray hair very handsome with his tanned skin and his bright blue eyes, not a strong face but a charming one, and it was easy enough to see why her tornado of a mother would have been too much for him, just as it was easy to see that on the rebound he had married Jill, a woman as soft as melting snow and without the strength he needed, and Jennie was simply too commonplace for him. He needed surprise and change, but these were to be only flowers upon the subterranean rock of a woman immovably faithful.

"And what," she asked severely, "have you to give another woman, Dad? Has that ever occurred to you?"

He looked surprised and, she thought, a little wounded.

"Simply myself, I suppose," he said. "My name, my house, et cetera. The usual male gifts, eh, Muriel?"

He moved into the area of charm, and she was quite aware of it, the inquiring humorous eyes, the deep caressing voice, the fluidity of his movements as he rose gracefully from his chair and walked about the room, filling his pipe and setting it alight. She was aware of it, but she was not touched by it. Long ago she had made up her mind that if she ever married—which she doubted she would do, having seen so much of marriage—she would never accept any man who had charm. She did not want it in the house, and now she spoke firmly against it, without mentioning the hateful word.

"I can't stay longer, Dad, because I am expected at home. But I want you to know that Joanna and I are watching you, and we are not going to stand for anything that will hurt Priscilla. She has the right to her fair share of you, as we had, though I always felt I was cut short, because you married Jill so soon and it was never the same after she came. She was always between you and me, without being unkind. She was always just there, if you know what I mean."

"Don't I just!" he groaned.

"Joanna was more fortunate because you stayed married such a little while to Jennie."

"You don't give me credit for not having married again before this," he said now, smiling to provoke her.

She ignored the smile. "Priscilla is used to not living with you, but she isn't used to having a stepmother here. We don't want her to go through what we both went through, Joanna and I."

He looked troubled. "Did you really mind?"

"Of course we did. But it's too late to think about us. Think about Priscilla."

"I've been a bad father, haven't I?" he murmured.

"Yes and no," Muriel said briskly. She got up as she spoke. "At least you've kept us in touch. We've had a stake here

in your house, even if it wasn't our home. I've got over everything now. I'm only thinking of Priscilla. She loves you
terribly."

"I know she does," he said humbly. He sat down and looked
sad, but that would be only for a moment, she knew.

"Well, I'll be off," she said in her dry fashion.

"Goodbye, daughter," he said. He was leaning back, looking
at her with quizzical eyes, where nevertheless some of the
sadness remained. "I can't say you've been a comfort exactly,
but maybe you've done some good. We'll wait and see."

She nodded, made a small smile, and went away.

After she was gone, she reflected as she walked down the
street, he would probably tell himself that she was too much
like her mother, then pour himself a drink and turn on the
phonograph to Beethoven and forget all about her. She knew
him well, and that was the way he was.

Her mother would not be home yet from her bridge. She
played almost every evening with three other women in the
same apartment house; one of them was a widow and the
other two divorced. The house was full of women alone,
though not always lonely. Some were young business women
like herself, but she did not make friends among them. She
had really only one friend, a small acid-tongued girl a year
younger than herself. With Liz she could say what she
thought, and Liz could be as frank. They told each other
the truth, that they both wanted to get married but not on
any terms. Together they planned their outings to places
where there were men. So far they had been unsuccessful
in their search, although between them, they had counted
up, they knew nineteen unmarried men, five of whom, Liz
said, she liked well enough to marry, so she would settle for
the first one she could get to propose to her. So far none
had proposed, for reasons which the two girls had analyzed
accurately. One was absorbed in his own woes and only leaned
on Liz when he was in trouble, one could not part from his
mother, one wanted to be a doctor and would not marry

until he was, two wanted to be career men in the army. None of them would Muriel have accepted. They were not hard enough in heart, not clear enough in mind. She had seen it all too close. One thing she never talked about with Liz was her father. That would be to reveal too much of herself and her wounds. She knew there were secret wounds and that it might be she was too deeply wounded ever to be able to love a man. All the deep tenderness in her nature was absorbed by Joanna and Priscilla, so long as they both needed her. Joanna was so childish, so much like her mother, and she must be protected until she married some man who could watch over her as well as love her. And Priscilla was so little that the woman in her could not yet be seen. The tenderness even spread beyond the daughters to the three foolish mothers, each foolish in her own way, needing a strong cold young daughter like Muriel to keep their accounts straight and persuade them not to spend all their alimony. Her father had been compelled to take out three life-insurance policies for them, lest he die before they did, but insurance would not provide for them as amply as the alimony did.

She spent a moment's pity for her father, a wish that somehow she could have kept him from being so prodigal of his money, that when he and her mother parted she might have held them together. But her only memory of the days when they were in his house was one of painful strain, she a small bewildered red-haired girl in the midst of two angry adults who waged their battles over her head, and avoided her that they might strike their blows at each other. She had been relieved when they parted and yet she had cried terribly when she and her mother moved out of the house.

Well, it was all over, she thought, sighing. There was nothing now but life, and life she had—a pleasant life it ought to be on so quiet and clear a night as this. The streets were almost empty of cars, and people strolled along the sidewalks, still hours away from tomorrow's work and cares. Nothing could be altogether evil on such a night.

It was at this moment that she met Angela Markham walking, she realized the moment she saw her, toward her father's house. Then he *had* telephoned her—he had found it too much to be alone after his sharp-tongued daughter left. Or perhaps her words had stung him enough so that he must see for himself whether he really wanted to marry Angela enough to defy his daughter. He was an impulsive creature, he acted upon an idea, a need, a longing, without waiting to examine it, and so he had called Angela.

She was hurrying along the lamplit street, looking rather pretty in a dark blue suit with white collar and cuffs and a small blue hat with white flowers and a short veil. Muriel saw each detail in one glance, though Angela did not see her. Suddenly she decided to speak to stay that swift purposeful walk.

"Miss Markham?"

Angela stopped. "Yes?"

"You don't know me, but I am Muriel Reynolds."

"Muriel—oh, yes!" Angela's voice was pleasant, neither soft nor hard, a detached kindly voice, just now somewhat cautious.

"I don't know if you even know of my existence," Muriel said.

"Oh, yes indeed," Angela said. "Your father has told me about his three daughters. Of course I know Priscilla quite well. We are good friends."

"I wonder if you would stop here at the park and let me get to know you a little, too," Muriel said.

Angela hesitated. "I'm afraid—"

"I know my father expects you," Muriel interrupted her. "I've just been with him. As a matter of fact, we were talking about you."

Angela looked surprised, hesitant, cautious again. "Perhaps for a few minutes," she said.

So they sat down on one of the empty benches. In a few minutes there was not much time, certainly none to be wasted, and Muriel crossed her legs, folded her hands in her lap, and began at once. "I don't need to know about you and Dad, because any woman who ever comes near him wants to marry him. He has suffered from his own charm. I really want to know now whether you are thinking of joining the procession."

"Is it your business?" Angela asked quietly.

"I think it is," Muriel said. "I'd like to protect us all from still another mistake, but especially Priscilla. I don't think she or the rest of us could stand another mistake. I don't know you and I feel I must."

The lamplight fell on Angela's face under the short veil. It was an honest face, slightly freckled, not an unusual face except in its honesty. Muriel rather liked the face, without being at all willing to yield to its appeal.

"Will you tell me in a few words why you want to marry my father?" One could put such a question to that face, and she did so, outrageous as it might be.

Angela looked down at her gloved hands. "A strange question," she said, "and I would be quite within my rights if I refused to answer it. But I shan't refuse. I have thought often about Morgan's three daughters. I have imagined a great deal about you and Joanna. I've asked him about you. He doesn't know you very well. As you've grown up, he seems to have mixed you up with his memories of your mothers."

"We are quite different from them," Muriel said.

"I am sure you are," Angela replied. "I can imagine that you would try to make yourselves even more different. I would not be willing to marry your father if it meant he would push you further from him. I don't love him enough for that."

"Then why do you want to marry him?" Muriel asked. She felt moved to defend her father though she knew very well he did not need it. "There isn't much money, you know," she went on ruthlessly. "He had to divide nearly all he makes between the three of them. He has to pay for Priscilla's educa-

tion just as he had to pay for mine and Joanna's. And if you
should have children—"

"As I hope we may," Angela said firmly.

"Well—" Muriel said, and spread her hands in a gesture
meaning, *You see, so how can you?*

Angela lifted her head. "I must tell you that if he asks me
to marry him, I will do it."

"Then he hasn't asked you yet?"

"No, but I think he will—tonight."

"Why tonight?"

"Something he said over the telephone. He's very lonely."

"And you were hurrying before he changes his mind!"

"Perhaps."

Angela did not look ashamed. Instead she turned her face
to Muriel's gaze, and the lamplight fell plainly upon her. The
lips, Muriel saw, were tender, while the eyes pleaded.

"You ought to understand," Angela said, "you are a woman,
too. But perhaps you are still too young. I am not. I am thirty-
three. That is not young. People talk about youth being as
young as you feel, but that's not true for a woman who is
not married. The young girls keep pushing up like flowers
in a garden and you see the fresh little faces—you see them
every one when you are my age, and you know you are not
young any more, not unless you are married and then another
sort of youth comes back. It's very hard."

The tender lips trembled slightly and Angela bit them to
hold them firm. This girl, this daughter of Morgan's, was young
and cruel. She would not understand.

"Then you are marrying my father just to be married,"
Muriel said in her cold clear voice.

But, her wise justness demanded, is it a crime for a woman
to want to be married? Isn't this what Liz and I have talked
about, and what Liz at least is bent upon? So isn't it a fair
enough reason for Angela to marry even my own father, pro-
vided she does him good and not evil? And there was no
evil in Angela, she felt sure. Oh, she had often enough dis-

cerned evil in women to know that here was a good woman.

Angela was speaking in a soft quick voice. "I am not ashamed to say I want to be married, but that is not to say that I don't love him. I shall love him with all my heart. Maybe it isn't falling in love. It will be love because it will be home and children and life as women want to live it, and he will be there. A man has to be there. And then it is the woman's duty—no, I call it joy—to build the home around him. I am not marrying him for myself alone. I am marrying him to build a home around him, *for* him. I don't need his money. I can make money, all I need. If he needs it, I'll make it for him. Money doesn't matter. But a man and woman together, that matters, and nothing else does. I am old enough to know it—and pay for it, when I see the man I can love." She paused and then she added a few pointed words. "And time runs short on a woman. The years for us are too few. There is none to waste, for me or for him."

She spoke so steadily, so quietly, that Muriel could not reply. It occurred to her that for the first time a woman came to her father asking nothing for herself except that he be what he was. Her own mother had wanted so much besides—she had wanted money and prestige, she had wanted to be *the* Mrs. Morgan Reynolds, but first then he must be *the* Morgan Reynolds, and he had not cared enough to be that. And Jill had wanted pretty clothes and furs and jewels and pleasures, oh, pleasures above all else, and Jennie had been stupid. Jennie had wanted to be lazy and eat and get fat. But Angela wanted the man to be what he was, and she would build about him the house of love and her womanhood. Into that house, perhaps, they might all come, his daughters, too, each in her fashion. Oh, she could see there was hope for it, with a woman of big heart.

The night was soft and dark about them, the people were going home now, her mother might be waiting, wondering where she was. Muriel got up from the bench.

"I've kept you a long time. Dad won't know what has become of you. Please tell him that we met and that we talked. Tell him whatever you like, only please tell him from me that everything is all right—whatever he does, I mean."

Angela got up, too, and they clasped hands strongly.

Muriel looked down into the good face, the sweet face. "Oh, but I must warn you," she cried in a low voice. "He is so restless—he wants variety—"

The good face dimpled unexpectedly. "I know that," Angela said. "It may surprise you, but I can be quite different one time from another. I have—call it imagination."

"Oh," Muriel said, not knowing what to make of that. Only she was sure that her mother did not have imagination, nor had Jill, for that matter, nor Jennie.

"I'd like to know more about that for myself," she said. "Sometime—not now, of course." She hesitated and Angela took the moment.

"Could you call me Angela?" she asked gently.

"Yes, of course," Muriel said. "Angela—it's a pretty name. Well, good night. I daresay we'll be seeing a good deal of each other from now on."

"I think so," Angela said, and went swiftly down the street.